JINGLE BELL BEARD

JULIE KRISS

The Kringle Family Christmas series:

The Grump Who Stole Christmas by S. Doyle

Very Merry Married by M. O'Keefe

Jingle Bell Beard by Julie Kriss

PROLOGUE

Jasmine

Seventeen years ago

Once upon a time, I broke a boy's heart.

I did it the week before Christmas, when there was snow on the ground outside our high school and decorations lined the halls. The semester was about to break for the holidays, and everyone was in a good mood. Everyone except me.

I'd asked the boy to meet me in the hallway behind the gym between periods, a move that was deliberate so we wouldn't have much time. I needed to do this quickly. If I gave myself time to think about it, I'd back out.

I smoothed down my cheerleading uniform and fidgeted as I waited for him. I had just left our final practice of the semester, and I was going to skip our last class so I could change and go home. Matt wasn't going to skip class, of course. He took school much more seriously than I did.

I should probably have been more like him. More serious, more ambitious, more smart. But I wasn't.

My heart skipped a beat when he came around the corner. For a second I thought it was apprehension, and then I realized it was joy. *This is a bad idea,* a voice in the back of my mind said. But I hadn't been listening to that voice all day, and I wasn't going to start now.

"Hey," Matt said as he came closer. He was smiling, something he did rarely—only around me. He looked as happy to see me as I was to see him.

This is a bad idea.

No. I was going to go through with it.

Matt didn't touch me, didn't kiss me, though I could tell he wanted to. And I wanted him to. He was a hockey player, and he was huge—bigger than the other boys in school, even the football players. He had a mop of dark hair and a serious face. He didn't talk much, except to me. He didn't have any friends, except for me. He didn't like anyone in school, except for me.

He wasn't exactly popular with girls, most of whom worshipped the football team. But I liked it when he touched me. I liked the feel of his big hands and I liked the way his muscles bunched in his shoulders when I put my arms around him. We hadn't gone all the way, even though we'd been dating for months now. Matt was a gentleman, and he was waiting for me to tell him it was okay.

We stared at each other, and then we both spoke at the same time.

Matt said, "Listen, I was going to ask you—"

I said, "We're not dating anymore."

A stunned silence fell between us. Around the corner and

down the hall, someone laughed. Someone else slammed a locker door.

"What?" Matt said.

I couldn't say anything for a second. I couldn't breathe. My chest was seized with pain. Why was I in so much pain? It was me who had said the words, not him.

"We're not dating anymore." The words came out of my numb lips, the script I'd written in my head and rehearsed.

Matt blinked, those dark eyes of his bewildered. "Why not?"

"It isn't working." Yes. This was what I had repeated to myself at the mirror in the girls' bathroom. It had sounded very rational when I had said it then. "You and me. We're too different."

"What do you mean?" His words were kind of choked, like someone had kicked him in the stomach. Like *I* had kicked him in the stomach.

"Come on, Matt." I waved at the space between us. "We don't fit at all. We're opposites. You're good at school, and I'm not. You like to read books, and I only watch TV. I'm the head cheerleader for the football team, and you play hockey." In fact, Matt was the only hockey player at Salt Springs High, which was a football school through and through. We didn't have a hockey team. Matt played in a local league and trained at an arena on the outskirts of town. "You haven't made it to a single one of my games this season."

"You haven't made it to any of mine, either. You don't even know the rules of hockey." The words popped out of Matt's mouth, and then he shook his head. "It isn't a big deal. Our schedules didn't line up."

"Our schedules are *never* going to line up." I sounded almost desperate, so I tried to calm my voice. "We're both so busy, we barely see each other. We didn't even do anything for your birthday." He'd had a game, and I'd been at a cheerleading championship in Denver.

"Jasmine," Matt said, his voice cracking a little. Then he seemed to get control and his voice went dark. "I get it. I don't fit in with your world. Your cheerleading friends make fun of me. Your buddies on the football team try to beat me up for sport. You haven't introduced me to your parents, and when my parents invited you to Thanksgiving, you said no."

"I was busy!" I cried.

"You stayed in town, just like we did," Matt said. "We could have seen each other, even if it wasn't a big family dinner. But you said no, and then you didn't answer my calls. I should have known then that something was wrong."

I felt my cheeks flush hot. I *had* made plans with my parents for Thanksgiving weekend—but not for the whole thing. I could have made time to see his parents, who had always been nice to me. I could have made a trip to the Kringle Christmas Tree farm.

"Well, you didn't visit my family, either," I said.

"The only member of your family that I've met is your brother, and that's because he goes to this school. I've gone to school with him for years, and the only words he's ever said to me are 'My sister is going to dump you, moron.'"

My jaw dropped. Okay, maybe Brad was a bit of a snob. He was a football player, after all. And he'd teased me relentlessly since the moment he found out I was dating Matt, asking if I was "still seeing that hockey goon." Maybe that teasing had gotten to me a little bit. I didn't know he'd said that to my boyfriend.

But I couldn't back out now. I was too far in. The only way was forward.

"You see?" I said. "We're too different. This was never going to work. Besides, you're already being scouted by agents. You're going to get a hockey scholarship. And then you'll be gone, and I'll still be here in Salt Springs."

This, I knew, was going to happen. I may not know much about hockey, but I knew that Matt Kringle was very, very good, even at seventeen. If I wanted to be honest with myself—which at this moment, I really didn't—the idea of it terrified me. Matt Kringle was going to leave for an amazing career in the NHL, and he was going to forget about me. We already had an end date. And after a few nights of crying and freaking myself out about how much I liked him, I had decided that the end date needed to be now.

If you got ahead of the pain, then maybe it wouldn't hurt so much. That had been the theory. Right now, with my throat closed up and tears in my eyes, it didn't feel like that theory was right at all.

"This is what you want?" Matt asked. "To break up with me?"

I made myself say it. I had to—he was going away, and I would still be here, going nowhere. "Yes. It is."

He bit his lip, as if he was going to say something else, but he didn't. He turned and walked away.

And so I broke Matt Kringle's heart. By spring, I was dating Gareth Green, the quarterback of the football team. Gareth had no plans to leave town. My brother really liked Gareth. So did my parents.

Matt never spoke to me again.

That was fine. I was fine.

It hadn't been a mistake, right?

Right?

ONE

Jasmine

THE PHONE CALL came as I was putting my elf hat on in the ladies' room. I was trying to stop the green felt from sliding off my hair.

When I saw the name on the call display, I grabbed my phone. One of the pins I'd put in my hat fell out, and the hat slid down over my left ear, dangling there.

"Hello?" I said.

"Jasmine? It's Kristen. Kristen Kringle."

Kristen Kringle, who was taking over the management of her father's business, the Kringle Inn and Christmas Tree Farm. Kristen, who had showed up at my apartment and told me she had a job for me three days ago. "Yes! Hi!" I said, trying not to sound too chipper. Friendly but not too friendly. At least I tried.

"Are you busy?"

I glanced in the mirror. Green elf costume, felt hat. Yes, I was about to start my shift as a thirty-four-year-old elf, working for

Santa at the Salt Springs mall. Times were hard, and a girl had to do what a girl had to do. "Not at all," I told Kristen.

"That's good. I have some good news for you, I hope. I liked the pitch you sent me. I'd like to offer you the PR job."

I closed my eyes and refrained from doing a little dance in my elf shoes. A job, doing what I was trained for in the career I was supposed to have? Thank God. Thank freaking God.

"Jasmine?" Kristen asked.

"Yes. I'm here." I made myself stand still and act dignified. "That is amazing news. Thank you so much."

"Don't thank me yet," Kristen said. "It isn't going to be easy, getting publicity for the inn and the farm this late in the season. Most publications booked their ads months ago, and venues for events are booked up. But I liked your ideas. I'm counting on you to make it happen."

Kristen had told me the situation when she'd approached me about the job. Her father, who owned the inn and Christmas tree farm, had fallen and broken his leg at Thanksgiving, and Kristen had discovered that the family inn wasn't doing very good business. Kristen, who was a successful businesswoman in New York, had flown in from Manhattan to look into the inn's business. She wanted a top-level PR person to get things moving again and save the business before the season was over.

That top-level person was supposed to be me.

I was a trained PR professional, but the last firm I worked for went out of business because of—well, unfortunate events. None of which were my fault. Still, the disaster left me jobless, and despite applying to every PR firm in a hundred-mile radius, I had struck out over and over as my bank account emptied.

Hence the elf suit.

I was working independently now, and Kristen had asked me to pitch ideas. I'd called on my cheerleading days and projected myself as competent, confident, and cheerful. I had told her that I could absolutely turn things around for the family business, and that I would work day and night to get it done.

Apparently, she'd believed me.

"I can do it," I told her over the phone. "Thanks for taking a chance on me. I'm ready to start."

"I'll email you a contract," Kristen said. "Have your lawyer look it over."

Lawyer? I had a hundred and fifty dollars in my bank account. "Um, sure."

"Can you start tomorrow? I'd like to see a more detailed outline of what you propose to do."

"Sure. I can—"

There was a knock on the ladies' room door, and then it squeaked open a few inches and Nick peeked in. Nick was sixteen, and he was my fellow elf. His green felt hat was also crooked. "Hey, Jas? You ready? Santa's waiting."

"I'm sorry," Kristen said on the phone. "Are you busy?"

I shook my head at Nick, then made a sawing motion across my throat, the universal sign for *be quiet or you're dead*.

"But I'm supposed to come get you," Nick said. His gaze dropped to my chest in my elf suit, then bounced back up again as his face went red. "We have to get started before Santa drinks too much. He's already uncapped his flask."

"I'll be right there," I hissed, and then I walked to the door and pressed it firmly shut, making Nick's embarrassed face disappear.

"Jasmine?" Kristen asked again.

"Sorry," I said. "That was just, er, the neighbor kid. Asking for some tea." I closed my eyes. *Smooth one, Jasmine.*

"I see?" Kristen didn't sound convinced. "We were talking about when you could start. I need your help right away."

"I can start right away. Tonight. I'll put together a list of ideas."

"Sounds good, but there's one idea you can cross off your list right now. There's no point in trying to involve my brother Matt. He won't agree."

My hand went sweaty on my phone and if I turned to the mirror, I was sure my face would be as red as Nick's was. She was talking about Matt Kringle. The boy whose heart I'd broken in high school. He was now a famous NHL player, known as Matt the Mountain because of his size.

It was true—to get Matt the Mountain to do publicity for his family farm would be a huge deal for the campaign. *Huge*. Like Matt. The problem was, we hadn't spoken since we were seventeen, and he most likely hated me, with good reason.

"Oh?" I said, trying to sound noncommittal. It came out like a squeak.

"I've tried," Kristen said. "Our brother Ethan tried. He's said no to both of us. He refuses to help. You two dated in high school, right?"

I was sweating even harder. "Yes, we dated." Specifically, I remembered how he kissed me and exactly how far his hands had gotten every time we made out.

"Ex-boyfriend or not, he was an ornery bastard in high school, and he's even worse now. I know you think that getting him to come to town is a good idea, but he won't do it. Forget about him and come up with something else."

"I will," I said. "I promise."

As I hung up the phone, Nick knocked on the door again. "Jas, can you come out now?"

I swung the door open and followed him down the back corridor of the mall as I straightened my elf hat. My shift was four hours; I would get through it, go home to my small studio apartment, and start brainstorming ideas for Kristen. For my *real* job.

I had lots of ideas. The Kringle Inn and Christmas Tree Farm was a great place, especially during the holidays. Sure, my timeline was short, but all I had to do was get the word out and people would come.

As I shepherded kids on and off Santa's lap and snapped photos, I kept thinking about Matt Kringle. Those few months we had dated in high school had been... well, they had been awesome. Matt was big and quiet and grouchy, which everyone thought was bad. I had just thought it was hot.

I'd followed him on and off for the past seventeen years, and he was still hot. He was also one of the best players in the league, almost a legend. If I could get Matt to come to the inn, take some photos, sign some autographs... if I could somehow get his number...

Forget about him and come up with something else.

Right. How would I even get Matt Kringle's number? He hadn't said yes to his own sister.

Oh, and he hated me.

But I had a hundred and fifty dollars in the bank, and the elf job paid eight dollars an hour. After this four-hour shift, I would earn thirty-two bucks.

I could not live on thirty-two bucks. I *had* to make a success of this. I had to impress Kristen. I had to be the one to turn around the Kringle business and make it profitable again.

It was either succeed—or fail forever.

I needed Matt Kringle, whether he hated me or not.

The question was, how far was I willing to go?

TWO

Matt

"THERE ARE two kinds of hockey players," my coach had said to me once, back when I was twenty-one and ready to take on the world. "The ones who can play, and the ones who are over thirty."

I'd laughed at that. Because at twenty-one, I was an idiot.

At thirty-four, I'd become the second type of hockey player.

Thirty-four wasn't old, except in hockey player years. I had been playing for most of those years, and I felt every one of them. My knees. My hip. My lower back. My ankle, which had been operated on twice. And, memorably, my groin, which had benched me for six games two years ago. No man, no matter what he's done in life, deserves to feel that kind of pain in that particular area.

I stripped and got into the shower to scrub off the brutal physiotherapy session. The hot water didn't help the pain much, but at least I didn't smell as bad when I finished. I banged the tap to turn the shower off, scrubbing my hands through my soaked hair and beard. I grabbed a towel from the rack, mopped myself, and dropped it, walking naked out of my bathroom.

I was in my luxury condo in downtown Chicago, where I'd lived for five years while I played for the Warriors. I had never paid much attention to this place; it was just somewhere to sleep when I was home, which was rarely. I'd bought it furnished and decorated, and I'd never bothered to change out the ugly abstract art on the walls or the sofa that made your ass hurt if you sat in it too long.

But I'd spent a lot of time in this place lately. Too much time. The Warriors had played me in exactly one game this season, back in early October. Then they'd benched me.

They said the reason was the strain in my neck from an injury during the playoffs last season, but I knew that was a lie. The real problem was my speed, my stamina, my ability to maneuver. The problem was my age.

So I was benched, making millions of dollars for nothing. The team had given me no timeline to get back in the game. They had given me almost no communication at all. Even my agent was taking longer and longer to return my calls, giving me made-up lines. *Soon. We'll hear something after Thanksgiving, maybe. After Christmas. Just rest and get into top shape if you can.*

If you can.

I caught a glimpse of myself reflected in the stainless-steel fridge as I walked into the kitchen. I was still the Mountain, big and hard with muscle. For most of my life my body had been a machine, one that I carefully tuned and pushed to its maximum. Even now, it was still a machine. Except—and with nothing to do but sit at home, I had to admit it—the machine was slowly but surely starting to break down.

In the meantime, the Warriors were having a killer season and were on track to get into the playoffs. Without me.

I yanked the fridge open, ignoring the waft of chilly air on my naked body. After years in locker rooms, I was comfortable naked anywhere, especially in my own apartment. I had expensive blinds on the windows, and it wasn't like there was anyone here to see me. After my last girlfriend dumped me—one of the many times I'd been dumped since the first dumping all the way back in high school—I was single and celibate as hell.

Which didn't improve my mood.

I pulled a premixed protein shake from the fridge and twisted the top off. I hadn't had a haircut in a while, and my beard needed a trim. It didn't escape me that I looked like a wild man, standing naked in my nice, soulless kitchen and downing the drink from the bottle. I could probably do something about my image. Then again, they called me the Mountain for a reason.

My cell phone rang, and I banged the drink down in irritation. Damn it. If it was my sister, Kristen, or my brother, Ethan, I was going to be pissed off. I was done telling them that I wasn't going home to Salt Springs to help revive the family business.

Kristen was worried because Dad had broken his leg, and our family inn wasn't doing good business even though it was the holiday season. She'd hassled me to come home and help, but what was I supposed to do? Leave my NHL career, fly to Colorado, and help Dad get to the bathroom and back? That's what money was for. I'd offered to hire as many people as he needed to help him out, but of course he'd said no. Just like the stubborn ass had said no every time I'd offered to put money into the Christmas tree farm in the years since Mom died.

I kept offering. Dad kept refusing. *Everything is fine,* he'd say. *I'm managing it. I don't need your money.*

We'd end up arguing every time. Mom had been the one to act as referee between Dad and me, and now that she was gone, we just butted heads.

Pretty soon I got calls from Ethan, too. Ethan still lived in Salt

Springs and was helping Dad around his busy lawyer schedule. Both he and Kristen wanted me to suffer as much as they did.

No. Just no. When was everyone going to get the message that I wasn't coming back to Salt Springs?

I picked up the phone, ready to chew out the person on the other end—and I realized I didn't recognize the number. Very few people in the world had my personal cell number, and this number didn't belong to any of them.

If a spammer had somehow gotten my private number, he was going to be very sorry. But I had to pick it up, just in case someone was hurt or dead. "Hello?" I grunted as I answered.

"Um, hello?" It was a woman's voice. "Matt?"

Something jolted up my spine. Alarm, maybe. I knew that voice from somewhere. "Who's asking?"

"Oh. Hi!" The words came out breathy, nervous. Yes, I definitely knew that voice. "I'm so glad I caught you. I'm wondering if maybe you remember me?"

Remember her? I must be crazy. Because she sounded just like—

"Jasmine?" I said.

She let out a breath in my ear. "Oh, well, you do remember me, I guess."

What was going on? Were there hallucinogenics in that protein drink? Because it seemed an awful lot like the girl who broke my heart at seventeen was calling me out of nowhere. And she sounded like she was terrified and happy at the same time.

Because I was surprised, and because I have no social skills at the best of times, my voice came out as a bark. "How did you get this number?"

The answer surprised me even more. "I work for your sister, Kristen."

"You what?" I asked. "Doing what?"

"I've been hired as a PR consultant for your family's inn and

Christmas tree farm." She sounded a little firmer now, not quite as scared. "We're putting together a plan to put the inn and the tree farm back on track for the holidays."

Back on track to sell it, was more like it. I figured Kristen had no intention of keeping the inn and the farm. She was too busy in her high-powered job, and Ethan was going to run for mayor. Just the family home was going to stay. That was fine with me. "You're a PR person?" I asked.

"I am. I've been doing this for my entire career. And I think the Kringle inn and farm could really be a destination for the holidays this year. It could bring people in. I have a lot of ideas."

She was on a roll, like this was the pitch she'd rehearsed before she dialed my number. I leaned back against my kitchen counter, feeling the cold granite against my bare skin.

It was poetic justice that I would be buck naked when Jasmine Collingwood called me after all these years. She was the girl I'd never gotten to get naked with. And she was the girl whose naked body—which I had never really seen—had starred in my imaginative fantasies for years.

She talked a bit more about how excited she was to work for my sister. It was definitely a memorized pitch. Jas Collingwood wasn't calling me because she had missed me for all of these years. She wasn't calling to say that she had never gotten over me. She wasn't even calling me to say sorry for dumping me at seventeen.

No, Jas wanted something. From me.

I crossed my feet at the ankles, stretching my naked body out, and let her talk while I thought about it.

When I'd had enough of the pitch, I interrupted her. "What do you want?"

"Excuse me?" she asked.

"You want something, Jasmine. I know you do. What is it?

Let me guess. You want me to come to Colorado, right? You want me to help you out."

The pause on her end was a brief one. I'd give her that. "Matt, it would help your family out. A lot."

"Uh-huh." I scratched my beard. "And what exactly do you want me to do?"

"It would be so easy," she said, still in the sales pitch. "You could do some personal appearances at the inn and the farm. Do some photo shoots. Sign some autographs."

"No, no, and no."

"What?" Her voice cracked. I wasn't following the script. She tried a different tactic. "Your family needs you. Your father especially. It would do so much for them."

"My family is just fine," I growled. "I offer to send money all the time. My dad still tells me how you're his favorite girlfriend of mine."

"I—Oh. That was a long time ago. Your father is very nice. But if you would just consider—"

"No. Are you married?"

"Am I what?" Now she was really thrown for a loop. I pictured her the way she'd been in high school—perfect body, straight blond hair, those sweet, luscious lips that were usually glossed to perfection. No one could resist Jasmine Collingwood, especially me.

Who had she dated after me? Oh, right—Gareth Green, the football jock. I had memories of Gareth and his buddies jumping me after school on a dare. Apparently, it was a sport to try and take down the biggest guy in school, the one who didn't play the sport all of the cool guys played. I'd been jumped a lot by those boneheads on the football team.

I had always won. And a few times, memorably, Ethan had joined in to help me kick their asses. Ethan always surprised people with how well he could fight.

"Are you married?" I asked Jas again. I hadn't kept up with her on social media or anywhere else since high school ended. First of all, I hated social media. And second, looking up Jasmine would have hurt too much.

I might be big and tough, but Jasmine had floored me that day. It may as well have been a knockout punch.

"I, um, I am not married," Jasmine said.

"But you were," I said, because something in her voice told me she was hedging. "So you're divorced. Jesus, you didn't marry Gareth Green, did you?"

"I don't think that's any of your business."

"So you *did* marry him." I shook my head. "Wow. Okay. How many kids?"

"None. We didn't get that far." She'd just admitted that she'd married and divorced Gareth Green.

"You married that dick, and he didn't even have the guts to knock you up? I hope you got something good in the divorce settlement."

"Matt!" She sounded exasperated. "These are personal questions, okay? I am calling you about business."

I scratched my beard. "Except it isn't really business, is it? Not if you're asking me to help my family and work with you. The girl who dumped me."

"I did not dump you!"

"That isn't how I remember it. I think the words 'We're not dating anymore' means you're dumping a guy." Damn, it still stung. I was an idiot.

"You shouldn't even remember me!" Jasmine shouted into the phone. "I was just a stupid cheerleader. You've dated Jenna Miles and Astrid Peachtree!"

I blinked in surprise. It seemed she'd followed my career—or at least my dating life. Jenna Miles was a pop star and Astrid Peachtree was a model. Both of them, like Jasmine before them, had dumped me. "I did date Jenna and Astrid," I admitted. "And no, you were not just a stupid cheerleader. Don't ever say that about yourself again."

I said it roughly, and Jas went silent for a second. I wished I could read her expression right now. In fact, I wished I could see her, period. I wondered what she looked like after all this time.

She probably looked amazing. It didn't matter what she looked like now. Jasmine would be beautiful no matter what.

Technically, I could go to Salt Springs anytime I wanted. I sure as hell wasn't playing hockey right now, and it looked like I wouldn't be until at least January. Which meant I could help out with this little project of my family's if I wanted to. Too bad I didn't.

"Matt," Jasmine said, her voice a little choked up. "You have to do this. I know you probably hate me, and you definitely don't owe me anything. But please, *please* help me out."

My spine straightened and I felt myself scowl. "Why? What's wrong?"

"If I don't pull this off..." Jas took a breath. "If I don't succeed, my career is finished. It's hanging by a thread as it is. I'm lucky that Kristen took a chance on me. I'm really good at what I do, but I *have* to make a success of this. I have to help turn around your family business, or I won't work in PR again. And I know both Kristen and Ethan have already asked you to come."

This wasn't a line. She wasn't lying. Jasmine had never been a liar, and she was telling the truth now. For some reason, she was desperate.

That made a knot form in my chest. Damn it. Was that a tiny shard of sympathy? For fuck's sake.

"I have to confess something," Jasmine continued. "I got your number from the contacts on your sister's phone. I snooped it without her knowing, okay? I stole information from her private phone. If she finds out, I'm already fired—that's how desperate I am. I know that if I can get you here when you already said no to her, she'd be impressed. And it really would do a lot to turn the business around." She took a deep breath. "So, Matt, I am begging you. *I am begging*. Please, *please* come back to Colorado."

There was a long silence after that speech. The fact was, even though it was entertaining to hear from Jas after all this time, I'd still planned to say no. Until this very moment.

Until she begged me.

Jasmine Collingwood *begged* me.

Well, hell. Now I was interested.

"What's in it for me?" I asked her. "What do I get if I put clothes on and get on a plane to Salt Springs?"

"I don't think there's money in the budget to pay you. I can check, but—Wait. You don't have any clothes on?"

"None," I told her.

"You've been talking to me *naked*?"

"Yep. Completely naked through this whole conversation. That's what happens when you call a guy who just came out of the shower." I pushed off the counter and stood up straight. "Come to think of it, I could probably use a towel. There's still water dripping down my abs and off my—"

"Matt!" She sounded a little breathless. I liked that.

"Fine," I said. "Okay, Jas. You win. I'll get on a fucking plane. But you know what? I'm going to come up with some way for you to pay me. And it won't be money. Relax," I said before she could sputter in my ear. "It won't be sex, either. Jesus, what do you think of me? But you owe me, and I'm going to think of a way you can pay."

"Fine," she said. "If you do this for me, ask for anything you want. Except for money and sex. Because I don't have any money, and we're not having sex."

I hadn't agreed to that second one. At all. In fact, my body rather liked the idea of having sex with Jasmine. It was all those years of picturing her naked—a kind of sexual conditioning. But I wasn't going to go there.

Not unless she begged me.

"I'm going to put clothes on," I told her. "I'll let you know when my flight lands."

THREE

Jasmine

AT FIRST, I was elated. My professional brain shouted *Matt Kringle!* And the little flutter deep in my belly echoed *Matt Kringle!*

I had to ignore the second one.

Then, when he texted me his flight details, the tune changed to *Matt fucking Kringle.*

He gave me less than twenty-four hours' notice of his arrival. This was a problem for me. Okay, fine—he was only doing what I had asked him to do. Begged him, really. But it was still a headache.

Because I needed Matt Kringle's arrival home to be an event.

There was no way Salt Springs's most famous hometown boy, our NHL athlete, was going to arrive home without fanfare. There was going to be plenty of fanfare—and all of it was going to make repeated mention of the family inn and Christmas tree farm. Which, by the way, was open for the season, since it was only a few weeks until Christmas.

So I got to work. Sitting in my small studio apartment, wearing old yoga pants and a Salt Springs High T-shirt that used to belong to my brother, I lit a professional fire under my laptop and my phone. I called every media contact in my entire contact list. I put together a press release and blanketed it out over email. I called an agency in Denver and arranged to get a few models to come to the airport decked in Christmas colors. I called a party store and ordered some green and red balloons. I even called a florist and ordered a Christmas bouquet that one of the models could hand to Matt Kringle as the cameras took their picture.

It would be perfect. It just needed one more thing.

I texted Kristen. *Need to talk to you ASAP.* Thirty seconds later, my laptop made the distinctive sound of a FaceTime call.

I answered it, trying not to wince. I hadn't thought she would FaceTime me. Now, instead of seeing me at my polished best, she saw a woman who hadn't showered in... Forget it. Who's counting, right?

Kristen, of course, looked amazing. She was what my brother would call a stone cold fox. The Kringle genes were strong in all three siblings. "Jasmine," she said from behind the desk in the office she'd taken over at the Kringle inn. "What's the news?"

I felt myself grin in triumph, shower or no shower. "I need you to come to an event tomorrow," I said. "Ethan, too."

Her eyebrows went up at my bossy tone. "Is that so? I'm pretty busy tomorrow, and so is Ethan."

"This is important. You're both going to want to be there."

"Okay, I'll bite. Where are we going? And what for?"

"The Denver airport, to meet Matt when he lands. He's coming to Salt Springs."

I had done it. I had surprised Kristen Kringle into momentary speechlessness. I resisted the urge to pump my fist, because I had to remember she could actually see me.

"You got Matt to come home?" Kristen asked. "For real?"

"For real. He's agreed to do personal appearances and publicity photo shoots for the business. He's even agreed to do at least one autograph signing. And he isn't charging a fee."

"He better not charge a fee, or I'll kick his ass, Mountain or no Mountain," Kristen said. "He's still my little brother."

"His plane lands at one o'clock tomorrow afternoon," I said. "I have the arrival details. And I've just gotten an email from the airport rep giving permission for my event." If the airport hadn't given permission, I would have held the event on the tarmac. Or on the side of the highway leading to the airport. Or at a gas station. Whatever it took.

"What event?" Kristen asked.

So I ran it down for her. The models, the balloons, the flowers. The press. Hopefully some curious onlookers and adoring fans. And in the middle of it all, Kristen and Ethan would welcome their famous brother home—a joyous family reunion.

All of it would get covered in the press. And all of it would mention the family business as Matt's reason for coming here.

Kristen heard me out. At the end of my spiel, she said, "Okay, Jasmine, I'll give you credit. Lots and lots of credit. You've impressed me. I thought there was no way Matt would come home."

Yes! My hand curled into a fist before I remembered again that she could see me. I lowered it awkwardly out of sight. "Thanks," I said, trying to sound casual. "This is my business. It's what I do."

"How did you get in touch with him?" she asked. As my face flushed, she answered her own question. "You probably called his agent. It's easy enough to get that information if you're determined."

I nodded mutely, not wanting to lie. Not wanting to tell her that at our last meeting, I had sneaked the number from her phone when she handed it to me and asked me to enter my own contact information.

That would stay my little secret. Well, mine and Matt's.

"He probably has a soft spot for you because you dated," Kristen said. "Matt doesn't have very many soft spots. Congratulations for finding one and exploiting it. Well done."

"Thank you," I said. "Do you want me to call Ethan?"

Ethan had been a year ahead of Matt and me in high school. I saw him around town occasionally, and he was still a hottie. The besuited, buttoned-up kind. Yum.

"I'll handle Ethan," Kristen said. "It's better if this request comes from me."

"Okay, great," I said. "I'll send you the flight details."

"Got it. And Jasmine? Keep it up. Great work. I mean it."

When we hung up, I finally did my fist pump. Actually, I jumped off my sofa and did a little dance around my one-room apartment. "I'm back!" I shouted at no one. "No more shifts as a mall elf! Bite me, Santa and your wandering hands!"

When I was out of breath—which was distressingly fast—I flopped onto the sofa and stared at the ceiling. Matt Kringle was coming. Tomorrow I would see him in person for the first time in seventeen years.

My stomach did a flip. I was going to see Matt tomorrow. The Matt whose hands had been everywhere on me, including—

No. This was professional.

And everything was going to go just fine.

FOUR

Matt

WHILE I WAS on the plane from Chicago to Denver, I did what anyone would do in my situation: I googled my high school ex-girlfriend.

Unlike most people, I had never done that before. I had never wanted to. After the day outside the gym doors, when Jasmine Collingwood crushed my heart in her small, beautiful hands, I hadn't wanted to see her ever again. I sure as hell hadn't wanted to look her up and see her potential wedding pictures, her potential happy vacation photos, or pictures of her potential kids as she went about her life without me. *So glad I dumped Matt Kringle in senior year!* Those photos would say. *Dodged a bullet! This life is so much better than the one I would have had with him!*

Yeah, no thanks. I got her message loud and clear.

She didn't want me. She wouldn't be the last woman to not want me, either. I had gotten used to that fast.

The first thing that came up when I entered Jasmine's name was her Instagram page. I gritted my teeth and clicked on it. I hated all forms of social media—the reason was right there in the name. *Social.* I wasn't a social guy.

Jasmine's page was public, so I scrolled through it. I started with the oldest posts. There was a post about her engagement to Gareth Green, including a picture of the ring. Then some posts about wedding preparations. Then pictures from the wedding, with Jas wearing a strapless white dress. She was fucking beautiful, and she was standing next to Gareth, smiling. I wanted to kick Gareth in the nuts.

After the wedding was a single photo from the honeymoon in Hawaii—Jas in a bikini, an image that would go straight into my sexual fantasies. Then nothing.

The next post was a photo taken by Jasmine as she sat on a sofa, surrounded by boxes. It was a shot of her stockinged feet up on an ottoman and a glass of wine in her hand. Her caption said: *Just moved into my own place. Cheers to freedom! #singlelife.*

I checked the dates. There were fourteen months between the wedding photo and the *#singlelife* photo. Her marriage had lasted just over a year. And she had gotten divorced ten years ago.

Ten years. I suppressed a groan as I shifted in my seat. I'd assumed Jas was married with a bunch of kids, but instead she'd been single for the last ten years. I was glad I had never joined any social media or given in to the temptation to look her up. If I'd known she was single, I would probably have done something stupid—like try to get her back. *Beg* to get her back.

I smoothed my hand down my tie, trying to keep my composure. I was wearing a suit. It wasn't my favorite attire, but Jas had texted me that there would be reporters when I got off the plane, so I figured I should look presentable. I'd gotten a haircut and a beard trim, too, because I was going to see my high school ex-girlfriend. I wondered what she would be wearing. It was unlikely she'd be wearing a bikini in Colorado in December, which was too bad. I shifted in my seat again.

"Can I get you anything, sir?" the flight attendant asked me. She'd probably seen me squirm in my seat. She gave me a dazzled smile that said she knew exactly who I was.

I grunted, then remembered I needed to use my words. "No." It was only after she had turned away and gone halfway up the aisle that I remembered to add, "Thanks."

I went back to Instagram. After Jasmine's divorce, there were posts of her having fun. Girls' nights out, a ski trip, a winery tour. There were also photos of her at various events she seemed to have organized for her PR career—a restaurant opening, a city announcement of a new park, a half marathon to raise money for charity. In every photo, Jasmine was beautiful, her blond hair soft, her smile genuine. She had always been a natural charmer, ready to have fun with any group of people. Ready to find the good in any situation. It looked like she hadn't changed.

I scrubbed a hand over my face. I hadn't changed, either. Jasmine, with her easy, happy glow, was the opposite of me. Still.

Maybe she'd been right when she said we didn't work.

She hadn't posted at all in a year. I found the name of the PR firm she worked for tagged in one of her posts and clicked on it. The page had been deleted. So I googled it.

"Oh, shit," I said as I read. Then, "Oh, *shit.*"

Jasmine had worked for a company called Rose Peterson PR, which had the clever initials of RP-PR. To google RP-PR was to find a list of disasters over the past year, each one worse than the other.

There was the restaurant opening that had gone wrong when the celebrity chef the restaurant was named after was cited in several sexual harassment suits. That was followed by former girlfriends of the celebrity chef claiming he had given them scabies. The grand opening of the restaurant had been picketed by protestors, and on social media, the hashtag #scabieschef had started trending. The restaurant shut down after a month.

There was the dog walk-a-thon that had somehow been held on the hottest day of the year. The whole thing had been cancelled when three walkers passed out from heat stroke and the paramedics drove them away, their overheated dogs on board. That one had been called #hotdogdisaster on social media.

And finally, there was the children's charity lunch for a thousand dollars a plate that a list of celebrities was supposed to attend. On the morning of the event, the tent it was to be held in caught fire. No one was inside the tent at the time, but it had burned to the ground. Somehow, the right people weren't notified, and all of the celebrities had pulled up in their limos, dressed to the nines, to find a pile of ashes doused by firefighters and still smoking. The press had captured it all. Some jokester had termed that one #pleasedontburnthechildren.

After that, Rose Peterson PR had folded, its website and social media pages vanished into nothing.

Now I understood why Jas had sounded so desperate on the phone. Why she wanted to impress Kristen so badly and pull this off. Why she had begged me.

She had worked for this PR firm, and it had gone under. Those disasters were part of her history. Most likely, no one wanted to hire her now.

I heard her voice in my ear again: *Matt, I am begging you.* I had to shift in my seat again.

I didn't owe Jasmine anything. I definitely didn't want to be responsible for resuscitating her career from life support. I would just show up as I'd agreed to, let some people take pictures of me, hang out with my family, and then leave Salt Springs again.

I'd go back to the NHL, play the rest of the season, and win the Stanley Cup. Because that was what I did.

The fires, the scabies, and the passed-out dogs were not my problem.

FIVE

Jasmine

"THE PLANE HAS LANDED," someone said.

I looked around the arrivals lounge. Everything was in place: the models, the balloons, the flowers. The press I'd invited had started to gather, and people passing by were pausing to look, wondering what was going on. I picked up the last two pieces of this perfect puzzle and made my way over to Kristen and Ethan Kringle.

They were standing together, chatting in a desultory way. Kristen was wearing a smart blazer and deep green pencil skirt, her long, dark hair cascading down her back. Ethan was immaculate in a suit and tie, his dark blond hair just slightly mussed. His eyes were blue and his jawline was so perfect it should be illegal. He even smelled good. I tried not to swoon as I edged near.

"Thanks for coming," I said. "It's almost showtime. I wonder if you would put these on."

I handed each of them something. Kristen shook hers out, looking at it with a critical eye. "You're serious?" she asked.

"Yes," I said.

Ethan shook his out, too. It was a Chicago Warriors hockey jersey, a replica of the one Matt wore to play. Across the back was the word KRINGLE and Matt's number, 22.

"No," Ethan said, his voice flat.

"It's part of the photo op." I tried to sound confident when I really felt like whining. Or pleading. "It will look so cool. You know, Team Kringle." I pointed to them. "That's you. Get it?"

Kristen's eyes narrowed, but she was the first to give in. "Team Kringle, huh?" She looked at the jersey again, then shrugged. "Fine."

She took off her suit jacket and handed it to me. Then she put the hockey jersey on over her expensive silk blouse.

"Ethan," she said to her brother. "Just do it."

Ethan sighed heavily. Then he slipped off his own jacket—Lord, he was almost as hot as his brother—and handed it to me. "Don't wrinkle that," he said. I nodded and wondered if he would notice if I buried my nose in the jacket and inhaled. Just once?

He put the jersey on. The collar of his expensive dress shirt and the knot of his tie peeked out of the neckline. Somehow he made even a mismatched outfit look handsome.

"That looks great," I said. "Thanks."

"He's coming!" someone said.

There was a rustle in the crowd. The doors opened. A few passengers spilled out, wheeling suitcases or talking on phones.

And then...Matt.

He towered above just about everyone in the crowd. He had been big at seventeen, but... Oh. Had he been *that* big? He was over six feet. His shoulders were broad. His legs and arms were long and powerful. His thick, brown hair was cut short at the sides and longer on top, and it was styled carefully. His matching beard was thick but well-kept, and it made him look severe. Or maybe it was the scowl that did that.

He was wearing a suit—navy blue, with a tie striped in his team colors, dark blue and green. The suit had obviously been custom tailored for him, because it fit him perfectly down to the last seam. The last inseam, maybe. Not that I was thinking about his inseam.

Fans started calling to him and snapping pictures on their phones. He surveyed the crowd, his scowl deepening. He ran a hand over his tie, smoothing it. Then he caught sight of Kristen and Ethan. And me.

His gaze fixed on me for a long minute, and I couldn't read it. He just stared.

I gave him a tentative wave.

Matt didn't return it. He just stared.

Kristen and Ethan approached him, and he was finally distracted. He hugged his brother and then his sister as the cameras went off. Then Kristen, God bless her, directed her little brother toward the folding podium and microphone I'd set up.

One of the models came forward, offering him the bouquet of Christmas flowers. Matt looked disconcerted, but he took it. He tucked it under one arm and stepped to the microphone.

There was a second of silence as everyone waited.

I had emailed Matt a speech for this. *It's just an example!* I'd said, when in truth I was hoping he'd say it word for word. Except it needed to sound natural, too. I didn't ask for much.

Matt glanced at me and I gave him a thumbs-up, hoping he could read my mind.

"Thanks for welcoming me, everyone," he said. "It's nice to be back in Colorado."

So far, so good. This might work.

Matt cleared his throat, trying to recall my email. "I'm here taking a holiday break. Um, with my family." He glanced at me, and I mouthed the words *the farm.*

"Ah," Matt said, turning back to the crowd. "I am here to help my family with the inn and Christmas tree farm that we own here. Outside of town. The Kringle Inn. That's what it's called."

Okay. Not perfect, but we could work with it.

"Matt," one of the reporters broke in. "What do you think about the fact that the Warriors have benched you this season? Does that bother you?"

"They didn't bench me for the season," Matt snapped back. "It's temporary."

"Still," another reporter said, "they must be pretty certain you aren't going to play if they released you for this vacation to the family farm."

No! He wasn't supposed to take questions. He was just supposed to speak!

"It isn't a vacation," Matt said, his scowl getting darker by the second. "I'm not on a yacht in Fiji, for God's sake. I'm in Colorado. In winter. Surrounded by Christmas trees and my siblings. That sound like a vacation to you?"

"Do you think you'll recover from the neck injury by New Year's?" another reporter asked. I was never inviting these reporters anywhere again. "Or the groin injury? Or the ankle?"

"My neck is fine." Matt was definitely angry now. "My ankle is fine. There is nothing wrong with my groin. Every doctor in Chicago has looked at my groin. My groin is fine."

"Stop saying *groin!*" I hissed at him under my breath. "Please!"

"Still," the reporter said, "the groin injury was—"

"Two years ago," Matt interrupted. "I'm telling you, it's fine. You want to see my scans? I'll show them to you. I'll show you my groin right now."

"Stop saying *groin,*" I said, audibly this time.

Ethan stepped up to the microphone, putting a hand on Matt's shoulder. "Trust me, you don't want to look at my brother's groin," he said smoothly. "You'll never recover."

Everyone laughed, and the tension eased down.

Kristen stepped to Matt's other side. "If you're all worried about my brother's fitness, don't," she added. "I plan to put him to work. I'm not going to let him sit around and drink beer while Ethan and I do all the work."

More laughter. Ethan took another turn.

"It's amazing," he said. "My little brother is going to do actual work at the family business. *For once.* Considering he hasn't come home in years while I did everything."

"I work," Matt interrupted him. "I make more money than you."

"Maybe," Ethan said, "but I'm the smart brother."

"I'm taller," Matt said.

"I'm better looking."

What was this? A game of one-upmanship between brothers? This wasn't in the script. They were supposed to be happy to see each other, a warm family. Team Kringle. Not this.

"It's funny," Matt was saying to Ethan. "I can't remember the last time anyone called a press conference when *you* landed at an airport. Oh right—never."

"At least I have a good personality, and I haven't been dumped by a supermodel," Ethan shot back.

This was a disaster. I was thinking of doing something drastic —like tripping the fire alarm—when Matt motioned to the model who had given him the flowers. When she approached, he politely gave the flowers back to her.

"Pardon me," he said into the microphone. "Family business."

Then he turned, grabbed Ethan's jersey, and yanked the hem over his head like they were on the ice.

And all hell broke loose.

The reporters shouted with surprise and pushed forward. Ethan—who had been at least partly ready for his brother's attack—quickly recovered and grabbed Matt's expensive suit coat, trying to jerk it up. Considering how big Matt was, Ethan was a surprisingly good fighter, giving as good as he got. In a few seconds the brothers had kicked over the microphone stand and were falling to the floor as they grappled. Then the crowd rushed in front of me and I couldn't see any more.

I was frozen to the spot, unable to move. The horror was too much. I heard Kristen shout *"Knock it off, you two!"* I caught a glimpse of Ethan on Matt's back, gripping him in a headlock as Matt tried to shove him off. Kristen grabbed Matt and he yowled in pain, bending so that Ethan slid to the side. A reporter pulled Ethan off of Matt, only for Matt to shout, "Don't touch my brother, asshole!" And the crowd moved in again.

Balloons were released, floating to the ceiling. Flowers were crushed underfoot. Models ran away, heading for the exits.

And all I could do was stand there as—thanks to Matt Kringle—my career went up in flames.

Again.

SIX

Matt

"IT WASN'T THAT BAD," I said.

We were sitting in the small office at the Kringle Inn. This office used to be Dad's, but Kristen had taken it over. There were Christmas decorations everywhere. I recognized them as Mom's. Mom had always decorated the inn growing up, and she'd also always had baked goods everywhere. Even with the decorations, it didn't feel the same here without her. I tried not to think about it.

Kristen was behind her desk, her arms crossed. She had taken off my jersey and put her blazer back on. I was on the sofa, pressing a wrapped ice cube to my temple where Ethan had gotten me good with an elbow.

On the other end of the sofa was Ethan. He had taken his jersey off, too, though he hadn't put his jacket back on. His tie was loosened and the top buttons of his shirt were undone. His hair was standing on end and looked insane. I was ridiculously pleased that my always-perfect brother was a mess for once.

In the only other chair in the room sat Jasmine. She looked pale and—there was no other word for it—panicked. Like maybe she was going to lean over any minute and throw up into the potted plant next to her.

"It wasn't that bad," I said again, because I felt like the world's biggest asshole. I wanted Jas to stop looking so upset.

"My stupid brothers," Kristen said, sounding exasperated. "This is your fault. Why do you have to fight all the time?"

Ethan and I reluctantly shared a look of shame. "It's our nature," I said. "It's what we do."

"I can't explain it," Ethan said. "I see Matt, and I have to insult him. He's just asking for it."

"And I see Ethan, and I want to pummel him into the ground," I added. "So I do."

"You *try to*," Ethan corrected me. "You don't succeed."

I glared at him. For my entire life, my big brother had been the perfect one: good-looking, charming, popular. And smart. He was a lawyer, and he was planning to run for mayor of Salt Springs. Freaking *mayor*. While no matter how smart I was, everyone saw me as the Mountain, a big hunk of stupidity who could barely string a sentence together.

I had two things on Ethan: I was bigger than him even though I was younger, and I was an athlete. Sometimes that got away from me. Like today.

I couldn't help it. He was fucking insufferable. And I always suspected he was our parents' favorite. He was everyone's favorite.

"You two! What are you, thirteen?" Kristen snapped her fingers, then pointed at us. "You. Ethan. Apologize."

Ethan rolled his eyes, but he gritted the words out. "Matt, I apologize."

My sister pointed at me, as she had many a time during our childhood. "Matthew. Your turn."

When Kristen called me Matthew, she meant business, so I obeyed. "Ethan, I apologize for pulling your jersey over your head."

"I suppose that's okay," Kristen said. "Now, both of you apologize to Jasmine."

Jasmine, slumped dejectedly in her chair, looked alarmed. She'd been overlooked during our family drama. "Me?"

"Yes, you," Kristen said. She looked more closely at Jas. "You didn't think *you* were in trouble because of my bonehead brothers, did you? You did a great job. It was these two who ruined it."

"Jasmine, I apologize," I volunteered. I was going to say it anyway. "You did a nice press conference and I wrecked it."

Jasmine's lips parted and she stared at me in shock.

"I apologize, too." Ethan apologized more easily to Jas than to me. "I was rude and unprofessional. It will never happen again."

Jas made a strangled sound, and then she said, "It's okay, I guess. You've been under a lot of pressure."

It was nice of her to say. Too nice.

"We can salvage this," Kristen said. "It isn't a complete disaster. I think we can do damage control if we—" Her cell phone rang on her desk, and she picked it up. "Just a second." She talked to the person on the other end of the line, surprise crossing her features. "Really? You're sure? Okay."

She hung up and looked at us. "That was Tiffani at the front desk. She would like some extra help for a couple of hours, because suddenly we're getting a lot of bookings."

"We are?" I asked.

"Yes, we are." Kristen went into business mode. "I guess the video of the press conference has hit YouTube."

Ethan stood up, as if he was looking for an excuse to get out of here. "I'll handle it."

"Are you sure?" Kristen asked, frowning. Ethan had worked at the inn as a teenager—we all did—but it had been years.

"Of course I'm sure," Ethan said, with his I'm-going-to-be-Mayor confidence. It made me want to punch him in the face all over again. "If I don't handle it, then Dad will."

"Dad can't do it," Kristen said as she and Ethan exchanged a look. "You're right. He'll try it, even on crutches. You have to take over."

"I'm on it." Ethan left the room.

Kristen seemed to think of something, and she pushed her chair back. "Maybe we're getting more customers at the Christmas tree farm, too," she said. "I'll go check."

"In person?" I asked.

"Um, yes." Kristen tucked a lock of hair behind her ear. "It's the best way to see for myself. Maybe this wasn't a disaster after all." She walked to the door. "Matt, get groveling. Jas, don't let him off the hook too easily." Then she was gone.

Jasmine and I looked at each other. I was alone for the first time in years with the girl who had broken my heart.

She looked good. Really good. Her light blond hair was tied back in a neat ponytail, and she wore a tailored white blouse that hugged her curves and a festive red skirt that swirled gracefully when she walked. She wore knee-high brown leather boots and rosy, understated lip gloss. She looked like a Christmas treat.

I tried to avert my eyes so I wouldn't stare at her. All I wanted to do was stare at her.

As often happened when I was anywhere near Jas, the wires in my brain instantly got crossed and I couldn't think of a single thing to say. I wasn't witty and smart like my perfect big brother. Who, apology or not, had deserved to be jerseyed.

"It wasn't that bad," I managed, for the third time. I sounded like a jerk, but apparently I couldn't help it.

Jasmine's cheeks were recovering some of their color now that she knew she wouldn't be fired. She started to look almost angry.

"Maybe it'll work out," I tried again. I lifted a hand to smooth my tie, then realized my tie was gone. It had been lost somewhere in the melee. I had no idea where. I looked down and realized the top two buttons of my shirt had been ripped off. My jacket had been stretched and I didn't know if it could be repaired. Sighing, I stood and shrugged it off.

I looked over at Jasmine to see her lips had parted. She was staring up at me, her head tilted back because I was so tall and she was so...well, tiny. Her gaze was unfocused, but when she caught my eye, she blinked.

"What did you think you were doing?" she said, remembering that she was supposed to be mad. "It started so well. You almost stuck to the script and everything."

Right—the script, which I was too stupid to memorize properly. "I'm bad at scripts," I mumbled as I re-tucked the hem of my shirt, which had been half ripped from my pants. "I'm bad at this stuff in general, Jas. It was a bad idea to ask me."

"It was not a bad idea." She stood up. "It was a really, really good idea. If it had worked. Which it still can."

"Are you serious?" I gestured around me. "We just went through a complete disaster here."

"Maybe, and maybe not." She put a finger to her chin, like a girl in an old-fashioned movie. Except she was a modern, very beautiful woman. My gaze dropped to her mouth, and I remembered how much time I'd spent kissing her in high school. She didn't notice my stare. "Kristen just said the inn is getting attention because of that mess at the airport. I think there's a way to salvage this. In fact, I think there's a way to use what happened to our advantage." Her eyes widened. "Everyone in the state knows you're here by now. I'll bet we can get crowds to see you skate on the pond. And we'll get a real lineup for an autograph session."

"I'm not doing an autograph session," I grumbled.

"Yes, you are, Matt Kringle," Jasmine said. "You agreed to come out here and help your family, and if an autograph session is what it takes, then you're doing it. Besides, you owe me."

"That wasn't the agreement," I said. "We agreed that *you* owe *me*."

"That was before you jerseyed your brother in front of everyone at my press conference. I worked hard on that. You need to pay."

"I already paid when Kristen gave me a nipple twist."

Her eyes widened. "Was that what that was? I saw her reach into your jacket when the fight started."

"It's her most painful move." I winced just remembering it. My nipple still hurt. "Ethan and I both learned to avoid it early. My sister is a menace. And her fingers are *strong*."

Jas bit the inside of her lip. I could tell she was trying not to smile.

"You wouldn't find it funny if it was your nipple," I said.

To my surprise, Jasmine laughed. It was a sweet sound, full of humor, and, well—joy. I felt its effects ripple up my spine. My hands twitched at my sides because I wanted to touch her. I had forgotten the effect Jas had, the way she lightened my spirits when she wasn't even trying. She made me forget who I was, made me forget everything dark and sour about life.

"You know what?" she said when she had stopped laughing. "I never even got to say hello to you when you got off the plane. So—hi, Matt. It's nice to see you after all this time."

I stared at her. She was so fucking beautiful. And I had been so gone on her. And here she was, saying hi.

Damn it. Damn it.

"Hi," I gritted out at last. "What do you want me to do first?"

SEVEN

Matt

MY FAMILY'S property consisted of a 20-acre Christmas tree farm, the Kringle Inn, and the family home. When I left Kristen's office at the inn, I grabbed my bags and went to the reception desk. There was a teenaged girl I'd never seen before working the front desk. Next to her, still rumpled with his sleeves rolled up, was Ethan.

Ethan was on the phone, answering questions for a caller. "Yes, this is the Kringle Inn. Yes, Matt Kringle is here. Yes, he's staying here." He gave me a glare that would have singed my beard if I hadn't been glaring right back at him. "I'll check if we have rooms available. No, you can't be put in the room next to his."

I approached the teenager, whose nametag read TIFFANI. "Are the cabins all booked?" I asked her. Belatedly, I added, "I'm Matt."

Tiffani didn't look impressed by this information. "Um, no," she said to answer my question as she slowly clicked something on her screen. The inn had some individual cabins out back, which were sold at a higher rate. They were supposed to be for honeymooning couples and the like, people who would pay more for a bit of privacy.

There was a pause. Tiffani looked at me, blinking.

"I'd like to book one," I said. "A cabin."

"For, like, how long?"

"I don't know," I said.

We looked at each other again, silent. I could maybe see why the inn wasn't doing a lot of business these days.

"I have to put a date in the system," Tiffani said. Her voice said she could not care less about what she was doing, or maybe everything in life.

"Fine. Book me until the twenty-sixth," I gritted out.

"Um, okay."

Kristen might be mad if I stayed for free in a cabin that would get a good nightly rate, so I took out my credit card. Tiffani took it, clicked a few keys on her keyboard with her bright pink nails, then handed it back to me. She said nothing about the name on the card, so obviously she didn't watch hockey.

"Number fourteen," she said, handing me a key.

I grunted and took it.

"No," Ethan said into the phone to another caller, his teeth visibly gritting. "An autograph from Matt Kringle doesn't come with the booking. Do you still want to book?"

I left him to it and walked outside with my suitcase. My nice dress shoes crunched in the snow at the back of the inn as I made my way to cabin 14.

I let myself in. I was used to these cabins, to the familiar, slightly musty smell and the chill in the air. There was a bed— queen size, just barely big enough for me—with a clean, tidy bedspread and a dresser. A thermostat, which I turned up. Along one wall was a counter with a coffee maker and kettle, the minibar beneath it. In the bathroom was a large soaker tub, probably meant to be a romantic bathtub for two. To me, it meant a bathtub big enough that I could sit in it without practically folding myself in half.

I quickly stripped out of my ruined suit and my wet dress shoes. I put on jeans, work boots with heavy soles, and a T-shirt with a Henley over it. I slipped on my wool coat and left again, heading for the house.

It was time to face Dad.

Since Mom died a few years ago, Dad had been here all alone, running the inn and the farm. Ethan had his own place downtown and he worked long hours. Kristen had her high-powered job in New York, and I was on the road nonstop with the NHL. Dad had said everything was fine, that he had no problem running things. I'd believed him—or maybe I'd let myself believe, because Dad was telling me what I wanted to hear. I was starting to get the idea that things weren't running as smoothly as Dad said they were.

Then he'd broken his leg on Thanksgiving, which made things harder still. And instead of coming home, what had I done? I'd offered money. Sure, I was busy—and preoccupied with the possible end of my career—but now that I was finally back here, I had an uncomfortable feeling in my gut that was an awful lot like guilt. Maybe Ethan had been a little bit right when he'd ragged on me at the airport. Should I have apologized instead of pulling his jersey over his head and ruining everything?

I did not like thinking that maybe I was a jerk, so instead I got mad. This was my usual reaction to the bad feeling in my gut. I felt myself fuming as I approached the house.

"Hello?" I barked as I came through the front door without knocking. The house was messy, coats and boots piled in the front hall and newspapers, plates, and cups scattered in the living room. The guilty knot in my gut got worse.

Without taking my boots off, I tracked snow into the kitchen. My father wasn't there. Instead, there was a strange man sitting at my dad's kitchen table, eating a bowl of cereal. He was dark and bearded, like me. He glanced at me calmly and put down his spoon.

"Who are you?" he asked.

The question was so crazy that it was the perfect trigger for my guilty anger. "Who are *you?*" I shot back in a growl. "And what are you doing in my father's house?"

"I live here," the guy said, calm. He picked up his spoon again. "Oh, I remember. You're the son who plays hockey."

Plays hockey? *Plays hockey?* I had two Stanley Cups and three Hart Trophies. Who the fuck was this guy to say I *play hockey?* Who the fuck was he, period?

He was tall, though not quite as big as me. Burly, tough maybe, but I'd spent over a decade playing hockey with tough guys. I knew which ones were city boys at heart, and this one had worn a suit at some time in his life. I'd bet my salary on it. "Explain to me," I said, "why the fuck you are in my family's kitchen, eating my father's cereal."

"It isn't my cereal." Dad came into the kitchen, maneuvering awkwardly on crutches. His leg was in a cast. The guilt twisted my stomach again. "Paul bought it himself."

"Paul?" I asked.

"McCleer," my father supplied. "I hired him to manage the Christmas tree farm all the way back in September. Or don't you remember?"

Had I been told about someone running the Christmas tree farm? September was very fucking busy, the start of the preseason, when I'd thought I had a chance at playing. Maybe someone had told me. I didn't know. "That doesn't explain why he's sitting there," I said to Dad, pointing at Paul.

Paul kept eating his cereal, but he shot me a look of death. He didn't seem intimidated by me. That made me even madder.

"He lives here," my dad said, pulling out a chair and lowering into it. His white hair was tied back in a ponytail and his T-shirt was tie dyed. You can't take the hippie out of the man, no matter how long ago the sixties were. Too late, I realized I should have pulled out the chair for him. "He's staying in Ethan's old room until the cabin on the tree farm is finished. His ideas have changed everything at the farm. He's been a great help."

Unlike you. That was the unspoken part of that sentence.

"What do you know about this guy?" I said to Dad. "Did you do a background check? He could be a convicted criminal."

The spoon clattered as Paul dropped it into his bowl again. "You know, I'm sitting right here," he growled back at me. "And I'm not a criminal."

"That's exactly what a fucking criminal would say," I shot back.

"What do you think I'm gonna do, exactly?" Paul looked around. "Steal some newspapers? The beer out of your dad's fridge? A Christmas tree?"

"How the fuck would I know?" This guy was a piece of work. "My dad's sick. You could take advantage of him."

"I'm not sick," Dad bellowed. "I'm just fine."

"You're on crutches," I bellowed back. "You broke your damn leg."

"I barely feel it."

Paul pushed his chair back and stood. He was pretty tall, but I thought I could still take him. My reflexes might be slower than they used to be, but they were honed. I'd just have to be quick, like in an ice fight.

"Your dad is just fine," Paul said.

"Oh, so you're a doctor?" I shot back. "A doctor tree farmer?"

"I'm not a doctor, but I've taken him to his doctor appointments. Unlike you."

"I can take him to doctor appointments. When's the next one? I don't need you to do it."

"I'm fine!" Dad shouted.

"What's going on in here?" Kristen came into the room, bundled into her winter coat. She saw Paul and her cheeks went red. "Oh, there you are. I was looking for you."

Paul grunted and rinsed his bowl in the kitchen sink. "What's up?"

"Um," Kristen looked at Dad and me. "I think we're about to get a rush at the tree farm. Because of the YouTube thing."

If Paul knew about the airport fight, he gave no sign. Maybe he just wasn't interested. "Okay. I'll go handle it."

"You can't handle it by yourself," she barked.

"Yes, I can," he barked back. "It'll be fine."

"Whatever." She looked at Dad and me again. "Matt, are you staying in your room while you're here?"

"No. I took one of the cabins." I was glad of that decision now. There was no way I could stay in this house. Before she could say anything, I held my hand up. "I'll pay."

"You are *not* paying to stay at the inn," Dad argued from his chair.

"I'll decide that, Dad," Kristen argued. She turned to me. "Matt, you're not paying. You can pay for your room by doing anything Jasmine tells you to do so we get publicity."

I pinched the bridge of my nose, feeling a headache coming on. "I already agreed to that."

"Everything," my sister emphasized, pointing at me. "You are all hers. You belong to her. If she tells you to walk a tightrope naked in the cold, you do it. Got me?"

"Got you," I mumbled.

"Bossy much?" Paul said to Kristen. He was zipping up his coat, a frown on his face.

"You should talk," my sister shot back. "Actually, I take that back. Don't talk at all."

"Fine with me. I'm going to the farm."

"I'm coming, too."

"Don't."

"Deal with it."

He dealt with it by turning around and walking out the door, leaving Kristen staring after him.

"Wait," she said. "Where are you going?" She left, following him.

So that was how it was. This McCleer guy was living in my family house, changing around the tree farm, helping my dad, and there was something going on with my sister. And he'd been here since September, which no one had told me. Or I didn't remember.

And my dad insisted he was fine, even though he wasn't. And I had a knot of guilt in my stomach.

There was a good reason I hadn't been back here for years.

"I'm going back to my cabin," I said to Dad, and walked back out the door.

EIGHT

Jasmine

"THIS IS GOING TO BE GREAT," I said.

We were in my car the next morning. I'd picked him up from the Kringle Inn, and we were driving to downtown Salt Springs for our first event.

"Sure," Matt said. He didn't sound enthused, but he was here, his huge frame overflowing the passenger side of my car. The internet said he was six-five. I'd looked it up.

The Mountain, an NHL legend, was in my car right now, wearing a black sweater and black jeans with a wool coat over them. There was snow in his hair and in his eyelashes because he'd been waiting outside the inn when I pulled up. His beard was thick and dark. He smelled like fresh snow and man, and I felt my ovaries do a little dance deep in my belly. I told them to stand down.

"We could have taken my rental car," Matt said. "So you don't have to drive in the snow."

"It's fine." It wasn't snowing very hard, just a few large flakes in the air that made everything look Christmassy. Since I had lived in Colorado all my life, I was used to winter driving. "They only gave me a parking pass for this car." I held up the flimsy piece of paper. "You probably don't understand the importance of the parking pass in my line of work. The parking pass is *everything*."

He looked unimpressed. Of course he did—he was a big-time hockey player who got driven everywhere and never had to deal with the Hunger Games of parking that was downtown Salt Springs at Christmas.

"I would have paid for a driver," Matt said.

I felt myself smiling as I drove. NHL player or not, this was the Matt Kringle I remembered from high school. Yes, he was grouchy, but underneath that, he was very sweet. I had lost count of how many times he had carried my bag for me in those days or brought me something I liked at lunch. He'd once gone across town and back to pick up my cheerleading uniform from the cleaner's when I needed it for a game. Why didn't everyone else see what I saw?

He'd been so nice to me. And I'd liked him so much. And then I remembered that day outside the gym doors, and I stopped smiling.

"Matt," I said, "I think we should talk about high school."

His reply was immediate. "I'd rather not."

"We should," I insisted. "It's been so long. Maybe we should talk about what happened after."

"I know what happened after," Matt said. "You dated Gareth Green. Then you married him."

I gripped the wheel in surprise. "How do you know that?"

"Do I have to tell you?" When I glared at him, he rolled his eyes and gritted the word out. "Instagram."

Oh, God. I had no idea that Matt was on Instagram, or that

he'd ever look me up, and suddenly I was self-conscious. What pictures had I put on there? Was I drunk in half of them? Please say I wasn't drunk in half of them.

I had definitely put wedding pictures on Instagram. Which reminded me—I should delete those.

"Gareth was a mistake," I said.

"You dumped me for him." Matt's voice was calm.

"I did *not* dump you for him!" This was the absolute truth. "He asked me out after we broke up." Actually, he'd asked me out *because* I'd broken up with Matt. He heard about it and made his move. I was so very stupid back in those days.

"If you say so." Matt's tone was disbelieving. "You dated him, you married him, you divorced him. You got a career in PR, and then there was the chef with scabies thing, and the dog walking thing, and the fire in the children's charity tent. So now you need me to meet the mayor. That's what happened to you after high school."

"You know about that?" This was getting worse and worse. It was pretty depressing that he could sum up my life since high school so succinctly.

Matt shrugged. "It's on the internet."

"Well, there's embarrassing stuff on the internet about you, too. Like how Astrid Peachtree is now dating your team captain."

Matt made a sound deep in his throat that told me he hadn't known this particular tidbit of gossip. "That doesn't surprise me. She likes hockey players. And she always had a thing for him."

He didn't sound too broken up about it. "Did you love her?" I asked him.

"No," he replied bluntly. "I got tired of going to events by myself. Plus, she's my height."

"Gosh, you're a real romantic."

"I play hockey," Matt said. "It's all I do, day and night. It's all I care about. Anyone I date knows they come in second. I'm up front about it. We do social events and great sex, and that's it. That's what I do."

Well. I was flushing hot, and I rolled the window down a few inches, letting in the winter air. Great sex? What kind of great sex? Like what specific acts, exactly? How does one make it great? Was it rude to ask?

I'd had sex, but had I ever had *great* sex? If you had to ask yourself that question, did you already know the answer?

"Okay, well," I managed when he didn't say anything else. "I just think we should talk about high school. I've always wanted to tell you—"

"Holy Jesus," Matt said, horrified. "What the hell is that?"

"What is what?" I peered through the windshield. "Oh, that's where we're going."

We had entered downtown Salt Springs, and Matt pointed to the huge green-and-red banner that was hung across the street. "We're going to that?"

I smiled. The banner said *Welcome to Mayor Ethel's Annual Christmas Jamboree!* Underneath it was a second banner, hastily handmade and written in black marker: *Welcome Matt Kringle, NHL Superstar!*

"They got the banner up!" I said, cheered up. "I didn't think they'd make it in time."

"You said I was meeting the mayor for a photo op," Matt said. "You didn't say anything about a jamboree."

"I forgot you've been gone from Salt Springs for so long," I said. "Mayor Ethel started the Christmas Jamboree a few years ago. For the days before Christmas, they shut down some of the downtown streets so pedestrians can Christmas shop. They have music, cider, games for kids, that kind of thing. And she makes a speech every year."

"Wasn't Ethel the mayor when we were in high school?"

"Yes, she was. I guess mayors don't have term limits, because the town keeps voting her back in. She turned eighty-six this year."

"Holy shit," Matt said. "No wonder Ethan is going to run to replace her."

"She's still sharp, you'll see." I turned into the fenced-off parking lot that said STAFF AND AUTHORIZED PERSONS ONLY. Cars honked at us. We were at the edge of the closed-off pedestrian area, and drivers were circling, frustrated, as they tried to find somewhere to park. "Aha," I said to Matt. "Now you see the importance of the parking pass."

"You're really excited about that," Matt said. "I should get you into a hockey game sometime."

"I don't know anything about hockey, remember?" I knew that Matt was a defenseman, and they called him the Mountain not just because of his size, but because it was impossible to get the puck past him. The name stuck after his coach said, "If you think you're going to score, think again. You have to get past the Mountain first."

"I didn't mean you'd watch the game," Matt said. "Just for the parking part."

I laughed. "A parking pass for the United Center on game night? You would make my year. Now you know what to get me for Christmas."

We parked and got out of the car. It was a beautiful December day. Even though he was dressed in black and wore his trademark scowl, Matt looked incredibly handsome. I found that I enjoyed walking next to him, feeling his size at my shoulder. I had enjoyed this feeling in high school, too. Just going places with Matt was thrilling, knowing that this huge guy was all mine and that everyone could see it. Not that Matt was mine now —but I still liked it.

We walked to the center of the pedestrian area, a square that was festooned on all sides with garlands hanging from the streetlights and sprigs of holly tied to the road signs. There was a raised dais in the middle, also decorated, with a stand and microphone. The press had started to gather in front of the dais, and volunteers wearing Santa hats directed people. Soon, a couple of volunteers appeared with Mayor Ethel, who was dressed in a red pantsuit. She was small and a little stooped, but her white hair was crisply permed and she had makeup and red lipstick on. With volunteers holding her elbows, she made her way up to the dais.

"Merry Christmas, Salt Springs," she said in a voice that was only a little quavery. "Welcome to my Christmas Jamboree!"

There was polite applause. Mayor Ethel went on, "I'm told we have a special guest today, and I'm going to give him the Christmas Key to the City. I don't need to introduce him, but everyone who follows hockey knows who he is. He's won two Stanley Cups and has made our city proud. Here is our hometown boy, Matt Kringle of the Chicago Warriors!"

There was more applause, stronger this time. Two volunteers stepped onto the dais and gently removed Mayor Ethel's red blazer. Then she lifted her arms and they put a Kringle jersey on her over her frilly white blouse.

I gave Matt's shoulder a push. It was like trying to push the North Face of Mount Everest. "That's your cue," I said. "Go up there. Oh, and Matt?"

He turned his scowl to me. "Yes?"

"Please don't jersey Mayor Ethel. She's eighty-six."

He didn't laugh. "Very funny, Jas," he scowled. "At least I don't have scabies."

That was a low blow, and it took me half a minute to come up with a comeback. Matt was already climbing the stairs to the dais when I cupped my hands around my mouth and shouted, "Are you sure?"

He didn't acknowledge me.

I admit, I was on pins and needles as I watched. I needed one thing to go right with this job—just one thing. Mayor Ethel made a short speech about how great Matt was, and then it was Matt's turn to speak. Since Mayor Ethel was only as tall as Matt's nipples, he had to bend way down to reach the microphone. He cleared his throat. "I'm very happy to be here," he said in his deep voice. "And I'm happy to be in Salt Springs." He glanced at me. "I'm here to help my family run our family business, the Kringle Inn and Christmas Tree Farm."

I gave him a thumbs-up.

Mayor Ethel came back to the microphone. "Matt, I hereby bestow on you the Christmas Key to the city."

Two volunteers handed her a giant candy cane—it must have been five feet long. It had a huge bow tied to it with scripted letters that said *Salt Springs, CO.*

Mayor Ethel handed it awkwardly to Matt, who took it in his huge hands. I silently begged him not to swivel and knock Mayor Ethel off the dais with that thing.

But he didn't. He crouched down to the microphone again and said, "Thank you, Mayor Ethel. This is a great honor." Then they shook hands. The mayor was not assaulted or otherwise injured. And the whole thing was over.

I felt giddy happiness bubbling within me. This was an actual success!

I had needed this to go perfectly, and it had. I could kiss Matt Kringle. A really good, deep kiss, if I was honest. I could do a lot of other things to him, too.

But for now, I'd settle for applause.

NINE

Matt

JASMINE WAS GLOWING when I walked back to her, the giant candy cane in my hands. Her hair was tied back in a neat ponytail, and she wore a dark green turtleneck under her navy blue wool coat with jeans and knee-high boots. Her eyes sparkled when she looked at me, and I had the sudden urge to kiss her. She'd looked at me like that in high school, usually before we dove into one of our hour-long makeout sessions.

Those makeout sessions had never gone all the way, but they were some of my favorite memories.

I was thirty-four now, not seventeen, and I had the feeling that making out with Jasmine wouldn't satisfy me anymore. I had learned things that would hopefully blow her mind if I ever got the chance to try them on her. Which I really, really wanted to do.

She was even sexier than she had been as a teenager. And I still wanted to see her naked.

As I got closer, I felt a warning twinge of pain in my hip. It was an old injury that made itself known from time to time, usually when I stood for too long without warming up first. The pain crawled through me, and I tried not to wince. I failed.

Jasmine's smile fell. "Matt, are you okay?"

"I'm fine," I gritted out. "I just need to sit down for a minute. Where do I put this thing?"

"Oh." She looked at the five-foot-long candy cane. "I don't know, actually. I didn't think the Christmas Key to the City was going to be that big. Are we supposed to take it home? I'm not sure it will fit in my car."

I winced again. "You figure it out," I said. "I'll just sit on this bench over here and wait."

I walked, I hoped with dignity, over to the nearest bench. I lowered myself down, propping the giant candy cane between my knees. Now it looked like I had a huge, red-and-green-swirled erection. I didn't care.

Damn my body. Damn getting old—at least, too old for professional hockey. Was this how it was going to be from now on? Was I going to feel every hit, every smash into the boards in my body? My agent hadn't called me since I got here, even after the disaster at the airport. I'd had one phone message from the NHL publicity department—*Don't worry, we'll handle the fallout*—and then nothing.

If they didn't care that I'd left town for a Christmas vacation, it was because they didn't plan to have me back anytime soon. Maybe I should just apply for a job driving the Zamboni.

I looked at the swirling crowds around me. A few fans waved and took pictures, and I tried not to look too forbidding. I gave them polite nods and waves in return without getting up from my bench. My hip was starting to relax.

Jas came back, and I watched her come closer through the crowd. How the hell was she still single? She was by far the prettiest woman here. There was something clean and sweet about her, mixed in with how beautiful her face was and how sexy her body was. Her skin was flawless, like cream. I still remembered what her skin had smelled like at seventeen.

She smiled as she got close, as if she was happy to see me. Her cheeks were red from the cold air. "That candy cane looks kind of dirty when you hold it like that," she said.

"I know," I replied. "I don't care."

"Okay, well. I checked with the volunteers, and we don't actually have to leave with the candy cane. It was just a ceremonial thing. They put it in storage to give to someone else next year."

"What a ripoff," I deadpanned. "I thought all these years in the NHL would pay off. I guess I was wrong."

"I guess your millions will have to console you," Jas said, "along with the pop stars and supermodels and whatnot."

"I'd rather have this candy cane."

She laughed, but in that moment, I almost meant it. I liked sitting here on this bench, in this cheesy Christmas square, nodding at friendly fans and holding this stupid candy cane. I liked breathing the fresh air and listening to the crowd. I liked knowing that I was waiting for Jasmine to come back and smile at me.

"I'll bring the candy cane back," Jas said, reaching for it.

"It's fine. I'll take it."

"Don't get up, Matt. I can—"

"Jasmine. I can walk. I'll carry it."

"Let me—"

We both had our hands on it. She tugged, and I tugged. Then Jasmine lost her balance, and we both dropped the candy cane. By reflex, my hands flew to her hips, grabbing her. She rotated and fell.

Straight into my lap.

TEN

Jasmine

I WAS SITTING in Matt Kringle's lap. In public. My butt was all the way at the tops of his thighs and my knees were hooked over his legs. I had overbalanced backward, and one of his big arms was curled behind my back, holding me. His other arm was braced under my thigh, his hand on my hip.

Well, his palm was on my hip. But his hands were so big that his fingertips were on my ass.

He looked as surprised as I was. His eyes met mine, and for a second we froze. How, *how* was Matt this handsome? His eyes were dark gray, like the storm clouds over a lake. His beard was deep brown and looked soft to the touch. A thin scar sliced one eyebrow, obviously an old hockey injury. He hadn't had that in high school. I wondered when he'd gotten it.

I wondered what it felt like to kiss a man with a beard. I'd never done that before.

He didn't take his gaze from my face. He didn't squirm, and

he didn't dump me off his lap. His thighs were rock hard beneath my butt, his arm huge and strong behind my back. The warmth from his body seeped up through me.

I wanted him to pick me up and carry me out of here. Then I wanted him to take me somewhere private so we could both get naked.

He knew exactly what I wanted. He could read it on my face. His gaze darkened and his chest rose and fell with his breath. He didn't speak.

He just stared at me, as if he wanted to rip all of my clothes off. And I realized—I *recognized* that stare. It was the same stare he'd given me in the airport, the same stare he gave me every time he looked at me.

Every. Single. Time.

Every time he looked at me, he wanted to rip my clothes off. Because he wanted *me*.

I wanted him, too. I should tell him that. I should just say the words: *I want you. Take me, you sexy beast. Take me!*

My lips parted.

Suddenly I was aware that we were in the middle of a crowd. We were smack dab in the center of the Christmas Jamboree, and we were about to combust.

"I'll get up," I said weakly.

Matt blinked as if he'd been asleep. "What?"

"I'll get up now. From your lap?" I was so befuddled it came out wrong. "Thanks for, um, catching me."

"Oh. Right." He grunted, and then his hand slid off my hip—reluctantly, I thought. His thighs shifted beneath me—holy hell, those thighs! Hockey player thighs. I wanted to see them bare. *Take me, sexy beast!* Instead, I rotated and moved off his lap to stand up.

"I'll just return this," I said, grabbing the giant candy cane.

Then, without looking at him again, I turned and fled into the crowd.

AT ONE A.M. that night I was still awake in bed, staring at the ceiling.

I was thinking about Matt Kringle. His scowly face. His broad shoulders. His beard. His thighs.

And I was thinking about high school.

Most kids felt lonely and alienated in high school, but not me. There was no other way to put it: I had been one of the popular girls. I'd been a cheerleader and volunteered on the Student Council. I was never pudgy and my skin didn't break out. Boys liked me. Teachers liked me. Other girls wanted to hang out with me. I got good grades and worked a part-time job at a movie theater, where I also did well. I was just that girl—I couldn't help it.

I wasn't a mean girl or a snob. I was nice to everyone, or I tried to be. My family had enough money, but we weren't crazy rich. I didn't have designer clothes or thousand-dollar handbags. I didn't gossip or backstab anyone. I'd tried to be a good person, but there was no doubt that I was spoiled in a lot of ways, used to getting just about everything I wanted.

The only flaw in my reputation—if you could call it that—was that I wouldn't put out. After I turned down my first few boyfriends, gossip got around. I was known as frigid, an ice queen. It sucked, but I wasn't about to start screwing boys when I wasn't ready at sixteen just to please a few idiots. So I lived with it.

The result was that I didn't get asked out much, and when a boy did ask me out, I always wondered if it was on a dare. So I focused on cheerleading and my grades and my job, and I didn't have a boyfriend.

Then I sat next to Matt Kringle in English class.

I'd known who he was. He was already taller than any other guy in our grade, and he was quiet and usually awkward. He played hockey when all the popular boys played football, and he had to play for an external league because our school didn't have a hockey program. He lived on a tree farm outside of town with his ex-hippie parents and his two older siblings. He didn't have many friends, and he definitely didn't have a girlfriend.

In my bubble of perfection, I had barely noticed Matt Kringle. I didn't look down on him, because I didn't have an opinion about him at all. Until he sat next to me in English class on the first day of senior year, he'd been just part of the landscape.

That first day, I'd noticed him right away. It was something about his size, his presence, the way he didn't try to chat me up. He didn't talk to me at all. I wasn't used to that.

Up close, I could see he was good-looking. I liked his cheekbones and his chin and his steady gray eyes. And even though I knew a lot of football players, I liked the raw power of Matt's body. He moved with lethal grace, and I wondered what he looked like on the ice.

The next time we had English class together, I sat next to him again. And again. And again. Wherever he sat, there I'd be, dropping into the seat next to him. He still didn't talk to me. It started to drive me crazy.

I'd never chased a boy before. I was too used to being chased, to being the prize. I didn't know how to chase a boy, especially one that wasn't talking to me. I kept sitting next to him and he kept not getting the message.

I became a little obsessed. I kept an ear out for gossip about him, though no one had any. I knew where his locker was. When

I saw him in the halls, I watched him without being detected. I did *not* like it when any girl came within five feet of him, but none of them paid him any attention. Matt Kringle was not cool, and he was given a wide berth.

But no matter how many signals I threw his way, he wouldn't ask me out. He'd barely even speak to me. He asked to borrow my pen once, and I nearly swooned. That was the effect this strange, quiet boy had on me out of nowhere.

One day, at the end of September, I was sitting next to him in class, like usual. The teacher had checked out and the class was killing time, so we were watching a movie instead of learning anything. The movie was a recording of a stage version of *Richard III*, so it was supposed to be educational. It was so boring my eyeballs hurt. I was way too stupid to understand Shakespearean language.

During some soliloquy or other, I turned my head to glance at Matt Kringle. And found he was staring at me.

It wasn't a casual stare. His gray eyes were fixed on me, unmoving. I could see his jaw clenching. The way he looked at me wasn't amused or assessing or anything else. It was *fire*.

I felt my heart speed up and my pulse pick up in my throat. I realized that in the weeks of sitting next to him in class, this had been the one thing I wanted—for Matt Kringle to look at me like that. Like I was the only girl in the world.

As Shakespeare droned on in the dim room, I leaned closer to him. I had one chance—just one. If I screwed this up, Matt was so shy that he'd never look at me like this again. Maybe no one would ever look at me like this again.

So I whispered three words to him. "Ask me out."

Matt blinked, as if he wasn't quite sure this was happening. Then he rasped, "Will you go out with me?"

"Yes," I said.

Just like that, we were dating. We talked until midnight on

our first two dates. On our third date, we made out for an hour. Matt was warm and sweet, and he tasted a little like caramel.

He was delicious. He was nice to me. And he never—not once—cared that I didn't go all the way.

I sighed, staring at the ceiling in the dark. My whole body was on fire, thinking of those days. Thinking of how it felt to be in his lap today. Thinking of how it felt to be around Matt Kringle, period. It wasn't the same as it had been in high school, and yet it was. I'd bet he still tasted like caramel.

I moaned aloud.

I'd have to tell him the real reason I'd ruined everything, the real reason I'd broken up with him all those years ago.

Just as soon as I got up the nerve.

ELEVEN

Matt

MY CELL PHONE rang as I was dressing the next morning. I'd had a fantastic sleep in my little cabin—it must be the Colorado air. My day was starting pretty good for once. Nothing hurt, and I wasn't fuming about my stalled career. I was almost in a good mood. For me, that was as good as it got.

It was my agent, Clark, on the phone. I picked it up. "What's the news?" I asked him, not growling for once.

Clark didn't notice my mood. "I could ask you the same thing," he barked. "But I already know the news."

I felt myself frown. "What do you mean?"

"Didn't you see? Jesus, Matt. First the airport fight, now this. We're doing the best we can for you here, but you're determined to be a goddamned train wreck."

"What are you talking about?" My good mood was going away fast. "I didn't do anything. I got the Christmas key to the city. It was harmless."

"Harmless?" Clark laughed bitterly. "I don't even know what I'm going to do. This is a disaster."

I was going to shout at him, but my phone pinged with a text. Clark had sent me a link.

I pulled the phone from my ear, clicked it, and stared.

It was from a local news site. There was a picture front and center of me sitting on that bench, Jasmine in my lap. Someone must have taken it on their phone. She was sitting right on my thighs, and my hand was on her hip. We were staring at each other.

The headline said: *Matt Kringle caught groping an employee?*

What the *fuck?* Groping? I squinted at the picture. My hand was definitely on her hip, but part of my hand was on her ass. I remembered how it had felt under my fingertips. Like heaven.

Groping?

I put the phone back to my ear. "What the fuck?" I shouted at Clark.

"You're in big trouble if this goes viral," Clark said. "We've never had this kind of trouble from you, Kringle. What's happening to you in Colorado? You've always been a stand-up guy."

"Everything about this is wrong," I said. "She isn't an employee. And I wasn't groping her."

"Fine, she isn't an employee. She's some random woman. And your hand is on her—"

"It's on her *hip*," I shouted. "I have big hands. And I've known her since we were teenagers."

"That isn't a bad spin, if you can get anyone to listen to it," Clark said.

"It isn't spin. It's the truth."

"Okay. It's the message we'll go with. We'll do damage control here, but you're going to have to do damage control there, too."

"Like what?"

"I have no idea," Clark said. "Fix it." He hung up.

I stood in the silent cabin, my thoughts spinning. This looked bad for me—really bad. No athlete wanted a story like this getting around if it wasn't true. It was the kind of story that could kill a career and end sponsorship deals. Not that I had any sponsorship deals—they weren't my thing. I was bad at doing photoshoots and commercials, and no one wanted to hire me for them.

But it wasn't just me. This looked bad for Jasmine, too. Her career was on the line. If she became known as the woman who got groped by Matt Kringle, she wouldn't be taken seriously ever again.

She was the PR expert, but I was going to be the one who had to fix this situation. I called her number.

She picked up on the first ring, breathless. "Matt, the news—"

"I know." Damn. She'd seen it.

"What are we going to do?" She sounded panicked, near tears. "This is a nightmare. And you weren't groping me! Your hand was on my hip! You have big hands!"

"It was on your ass a little bit," I admitted, because I wanted to be honest with Jasmine. "Sorry about that. I couldn't help myself."

"I liked it." Her voice cracked. "But this is horrible. For both of us. Everyone is going to think you're an asshole and I got groped. I don't know what to do."

For the first time, she sounded defeated. My indestructible Jasmine, my ray of sunshine, the most optimistic and resilient woman I'd ever known. There was no way in a thousand fucking years I'd let her feel defeated. "It's okay, babe," I said, my voice soft. "Don't worry about it. Everything will be fine. I have the answer."

"How, Matt?" she cried. "What answer?"

"It's easy," I said. "We're dating."

I MET her downtown a few hours later. I'd had to spend some time making phone calls, and then I'd insisted on driving myself instead of making her chauffeur me. I didn't want her to look like my employee.

Jasmine was right about the parking pass thing, which meant I spent too long driving down side streets, looking for somewhere to park. By the time I got to our meeting place, I was fifteen minutes late. Jasmine was standing at the entrance to a small downtown park, looking tired and worried that I wouldn't show.

She was wearing her brown knee-high boots and a coat that was belted at the waist. Her blond hair was down around her shoulders and her hands were in her pockets, her posture tense. For some reason, seeing Jasmine stressed made all of my own usual stress drain out of me. I strode toward her, feeling more confident than I had in a while.

She looked relieved when she saw me. Then her gaze moved up and down me—dark coat, black pants, black boots—and her expression changed. There was lust in that expression, and appreciation, and some kind of sadness. I wondered why.

I didn't bother greeting her. Instead, when I got close, I held out my hand.

She looked at my hand, then tentatively put hers in mine. Her hand was small and warm as I closed my fingers around it. We started walking.

"I hope you know what you're doing," she said as we strolled into the park.

"I know what I'm doing," I replied.

"You're not a PR professional."

"No, but I've been in the spotlight for fifteen years. I know people who know people. I can make an image happen, just like you can."

"Are you sure?" she asked, her voice tentative. "If this backfires—"

I squeezed her hand in mine. "Jasmine, let me help for once."

She was quiet at that. We walked slowly through the park, which smelled like snow and pine trees. The park was full of Christmas lights, though they weren't on in the middle of the day. At night, every tree and bush would be lit up.

It was a pretty place. And there were a few dozen people here. One of whom had been assigned to take pictures of us holding hands and acting like a couple, so the photos could be "leaked" online. And there you had it—proof that Matt Kringle had a new girlfriend, not an employee he'd groped. I didn't know which person was supposed to take the picture, so I wouldn't be tempted to look at them. Instead, I could walk through the park with my so-called girlfriend and act natural.

"You really don't know who it is?" Jasmine asked in a stage whisper. She was only going along with this because she hadn't come up with a better idea.

"Nope," I said. I was in a curiously good mood, considering I was doing damage control so I didn't get a reputation as a creep. Maybe it was because I was holding Jasmine's hand. "I have no idea. I talked to someone who talked to someone—I didn't hire the person directly. It works better that way."

"And you don't mind it getting out that we're dating? I'm not a pop star or a supermodel."

"Jasmine."

"Sorry. I'm very nervous. What's the plan? Do we break up after Christmas, before you go back to Chicago? Or do we pretend we have a long-distance relationship?"

We never break up, I thought. I had been holding her hand for less than two minutes; I wasn't ready to get dumped again. But what I said was, "We'll play it by ear. Okay?"

"Okay." She was quiet as we walked a circuit of the park, hand in hand. "Do you think the person is here now?"

"Probably."

"Should we keep walking a little longer?"

"Yes."

Another brief moment of silence. Then, "Are we being convincing enough, do you think?"

I sighed. "No. We're not."

"Oh." Now Jasmine sounded worried again. "What should we do?"

We were at the center of the park, by a snow-covered cluster of evergreen trees. Christmas shoppers were passing by and kids were laughing. It was a perfect Christmas moment.

I stopped walking and turned to Jasmine, tugging her toward me. "We do this," I said. I cupped her jaw and kissed her.

She froze in surprise for a second, but it didn't take her long. She kissed me back, slow and tentative at first, her lips exploring mine. Then she rose on her toes and kissed me deeper, parting her lips.

I brushed my thumb over her cheek and took the invitation. I was kissing Jasmine Collingwood again after seventeen years, drinking in her sweet lips and her creamy skin. Except this time, I wasn't a teenaged novice. I swept my tongue into her mouth like a man who knows what he's doing, like a man who's waited years. I explored her, licking her slowly and persuasively, as she moaned against my mouth.

Her hands slid under my coat and wandered my chest and stomach as I cupped her jaw. Her palms rubbed over my Henley, then lifted it and explored the bare skin beneath. She was practically shoving my shirt off right here in the park, and I didn't care.

We came up for air, reluctantly breaking the kiss. We didn't let each other go.

Jasmine's eyes were wide, her pupils dark. "Do you think that was good enough?" she breathed.

"Not sure," I grunted back. "Better keep putting on a show."

I lowered my mouth to hers again and we devoured each other. Jasmine wasn't a novice anymore either, but she wasn't incredibly experienced. She'd been married to Gareth fucking Green. I was suddenly determined to make her forget his name.

Her fingertips moved through the hair on my chest, then down my happy trail to my belly button, invisible to everyone else under the flaps of my coat. I kept kissing her, taking my time, leaving no part of her sweet mouth unexplored, unclaimed by me. I was in no hurry. I could kiss Jasmine Collingwood all fucking day.

And I could probably fuck her nonstop for a week. If I got the chance, that was.

Someone whistled, a few people clapped, and I heard someone say, "Is that Matt Kringle?" I probably hadn't needed to hire the incognito photographer. There would be pictures of this on the internet anyway.

Eventually, I let Jasmine go. She took her hands out from under my shirt—reluctantly—and stood back, her hair tousled and her expression dazed.

"That, um, probably worked," she said.

"Sure it did," I replied. "Let's go get lunch."

TWELVE

Jasmine

"I SHOULD GIVE A STATEMENT," I said.

We were sitting in a cozy diner in downtown Salt Springs. Some of the people here obviously recognized Matt, though most of them didn't say anything. We'd only been interrupted once by the parents of a ten-year-old boy who apologized as they asked for Matt's autograph. He had agreeably signed the boy's napkin and posed for a selfie without a word of complaint. He'd almost smiled.

Then we'd ordered lunch. I was too nervous to do anything but pick at my chicken salad, while Matt had inhaled a roast beef sandwich that looked like it weighed as much as my head. Apparently it took a lot of calories to keep a man as big as Matt fueled for a day.

And he was definitely big. He was the Mountain, after all. His body had felt massive against mine when he kissed me, and those hands...

I put a bite of chicken in my mouth. I could feel myself blushing.

Matt didn't seem to notice. "There's no need for you to make a statement," he said.

"But I'm the one who was supposedly groped," I said. "I need to say something official."

"I already made an official statement."

I put my fork down. "You what?"

Matt had devoured the sandwich, but he hadn't touched his french fries. He opened a packet of mayo, put it on his plate, and slid it toward me.

Damn it. I still liked french fries dunked in mayo, and he knew it. I stared at the plate, trying to resist. I was supposed to be eating chicken salad.

"Don't distract me," I said, tearing my gaze away from the French fries. "What do you mean, you made a statement? I'm the PR person. That's my job."

"Do you know how many PR people work for the NHL?" Matt put a fingertip to his plate and edged it half an inch closer to me. Then another half inch. "I got one of them to put out a statement to the press about my new girlfriend."

"I should be the one to do that," I said.

"No, because the statement is *about* you. Reporters pick up the phone when the NHL calls. Don't worry, I told them what to say. And I read it over before it was released." He moved the plate so that it clicked against my salad bowl and moved it out of the way.

I sighed and picked up a fry, dunking it and devouring it. "Am I angry at you?" I asked him, because I honestly didn't know.

"I'm trying to help," Matt said.

"By taking over," I offered, still eating the fries.

"I'm not taking over. It was just this one thing. I was the one who got you into this mess by grabbing your ass—"

"Unintentionally."

Matt shrugged. "The jury's out on that. Your ass is a magnet to me. There may have been *some* intention."

I felt myself smiling, despite everything. He was just so sweet under all of that gruffness. "I'm going to take that as a compliment."

He scowled again. "If you want. What I was saying was, I got you into this mess, so I made some calls and cleaned it up. Now you're in charge again."

I scooped the last of the mayo with a french fry. "You mean it? I'm completely in charge?"

He held up his hands. "I am all yours. Direct me at your will."

Oh, lord. *That* was a loaded idea. First, I would like to direct him to strip. Then I'd direct him to take all of my clothes off. And *then* I'd direct him to demonstrate to me what *great sex* was. In detail. With all of the positions. So that I could be completely sure I'd never had it before.

"Jasmine?" Matt said.

I tried to make my head stop spinning. "Sorry." It didn't matter that he'd kissed me stupid this morning. It didn't matter that I now knew what he tasted like and how warm he was when he put his arms around me, or that I finally knew what it felt like to kiss a man with a beard (the answer was *very nice*). I had to try and take charge of the situation again. I had to make a plan.

"Okay," I managed after a moment of thought, "we have to keep up the new girlfriend thing, at least until Christmas. So it's good that a lot of people saw us here today. We should probably do other things, too."

"We should go out to dinner," Matt suggested.

"Right. Somewhere where people will see us. Somewhere romantic."

Matt's gaze was fixed on me. "And we should act like a couple when we go."

My throat was dry. I took a sip of my club soda. "That is probably advisable. You know, in case we get photographed."

"Okay," Matt said. He seemed to be watching my mouth as I sipped from my straw. "And it's probably advisable that we also go home together after this dinner. So that people know it's for real and not for show."

My head was spinning again. "Oh, really?"

He shrugged his big shoulders. "I have one of the cabins at the inn. It's nice and private."

Were we actually talking about this? Of course no reporter was going to follow us from our dinner just to see if we went home together. That was the kind of treatment given to the Royal Family, not a hockey player hanging out with his girlfriend in his hometown. Me going to Matt's cabin would definitely not be news, which meant it wasn't required.

Which meant that Matt was hitting on me. Under the table, my toes curled in my boots and I tried not to squirm.

"I have the feeling we wouldn't be playing Scrabble or watching *Gilmore Girls,*" I said, naming two of the activities we'd done when we were dating. The first one was his idea, and the second one was mine, though Matt had never complained about my TV choices.

Matt's gaze was smoldering now. "It's up to you, Jas," he said. "You're not married to Gareth Green anymore. You haven't been for a long time."

Yes. He was definitely hitting on me.

I was a free woman, free to have flings or one-night stands whenever I wanted. Which hadn't been all that often, because I had been so focused on my career. And I hadn't dated much, because Salt Springs had a lot of college students and old ex-hippies instead of eligible men. I met nice guys at work events from time to time, and sometimes they asked me out, but everything had felt so...shallow with them. Like our entire relationship was on the surface. It was easy, but it was also never serious. It was just about appearances. A little like Matt and the supermodel he dated because she was his height.

Matt and I had never been on the surface. What I'd had with him, as short as it had been, had always felt deep and important. And the way he was looking at me now... I might incinerate right here in this diner.

What was I thinking? He wasn't just Matt the Mountain, hot NHL player and my ex-boyfriend. He was the subject of my PR campaign, the one that would either make or sink my career. And he was only in town for a little while.

"When do you go back to Chicago?" I asked, breaking the smolder that had heated the air between us. "Before New Year's, or after?"

Matt blinked, and then he frowned, as if the topic made him mad. "I don't know," he said. "I haven't heard."

"Well, they're going to want you back." I tried to sound businesslike. "You're Matt the Mountain, one of their big players. You won't be in Salt Springs very long."

"Maybe not," Matt said. "What's your point?"

"My point?" I tried to glare at him, even though my knees were still goo under the table. "My *point* is that I don't have much time to keep this campaign going and save your family business. So I need to make the most use of you while I have you."

He nodded. "Got it. So we skip the dinner and go straight to my cabin." He checked his watch. "Let's go right now."

"*Matt.*" I was exasperated and panicked and yes, not a little horny. Matt Kringle always made me feel all three of those things. "This is important to me. My career is important to me."

"I know." His voice was quiet.

"Good. So I want you to skate. I want an autograph session tomorrow. And I want a photo shoot."

He scratched his beard, and oh hell, just the sound of that did nothing to alleviate my horniness. "What kind of photo shoot?" he asked.

"On the frozen pond behind the tree farm," I said. "You used to skate there as a kid, right?"

Matt nodded. He'd told me that in high school. "It's where I learned. Taught myself with a pair of secondhand skates."

"See? That's perfect," I said, while my heart tried to squeeze out of my chest at the thought of Matt as a kid, skating determinedly on the pond, all alone, destined for greatness. "We'll shoot you skating on the pond you learned on as a kid. The photos will go up on Instagram and Twitter, with the inn and farm tagged. It'll be perfect. We'll even have a hashtag."

"A hashtag." Matt winced as if the word physically hurt him.

"Yes, a hashtag," I repeated. "That's my domain. You have a Twitter and Instagram account, right? The NHL must have made you at least claim your name."

He still looked like he had swallowed something bad. "Yes. I have an Instagram account. And a Twitter thing."

I pulled out my phone and quickly opened Instagram. I typed in Matt's name and found his account, complete with blue check mark. I tapped it open.

"Matt!" I cried when I saw his account.

"I don't like social media," Matt said.

His account had no posts. Zero. And it had two point five million followers.

Two point five million.

Twitter had the same name, the same blue check mark, the same lack of posts. One point two million followers.

It was ridiculous, but the PR pro in me also knew it was perfect. Amazing, actually. A once-in-a-lifetime opportunity.

Millions of people were waiting, right now, for Matt the Mountain Kringle to post something—anything at all.

He was going to post his photos, and he was going to say he was at the Kringle Inn and Christmas Tree Farm.

It was going to be the biggest score of my career.

THIRTEEN

Matt

WHEN I WALKED into the lobby of the inn, there was a crowd. Families, teenagers, kids—there were people everywhere, all trying to get at the reservation desk. Tiffani was nowhere to be seen. At the front of the line was a man complaining loudly while wearing a Warriors jersey. He was yelling at Ethan, who was manning the front desk by himself. Ethan was smiling politely, but I knew my brother. He was thinking, very seriously, about murder.

Ethan hadn't seen me, and neither had anyone else. I looked around and saw more Warriors jerseys, and even one guy in face paint. People were asking where I was, if they could get a room next to mine. Jesus Christ. I wanted no part of this scene, so I turned to leave. And I nearly walked into the sexiest woman I had ever seen.

Of course, Jasmine Collingwood was the sexiest woman I had ever seen. I had particular tastes. But the woman coming through the front doors wore her sexiness like a showy fur coat—all the way from her platinum hair, down her curves to her miniscule jean skirt and cowboy boots. She was wearing a pink trench coat that was way too cold for winter in Colorado, wheeling a suitcase, and—incredibly—she carried a bag over her shoulder with a dog in it. An actual dog. It was small, and it glared at me with hostility.

I took a shred of pity on Ethan and caught the woman's gaze before she could add to the crowd in the lobby. "Can I help you?" I asked her.

The woman turned toward me. She had a perfect face that had no need for makeup, though she wore plenty. Her lips were full and very glossy, and when she smiled at me I forgot my name for half a second. Then I remembered it again.

I had met a lot of incredibly beautiful women in my life. I had dated some of them and slept with them, too. This woman wasn't a supermodel, but she had an earthy beauty that probably brought men to their knees on a regular basis. Men who weren't as immune as I was.

"Well?" I asked her.

She looked me up and down. "You must be the hockey player brother."

What the hell? I had no time for this.

"I get that a lot," I said to her. "Are you with the Paul Bunyan asshole? Because both of you can fuck off."

She blinked her dark lashes and looked confused, and it wasn't an act. "What?"

"We're probably full up," I said. "You can't stay in the main house, because there's already some dick I don't know staying there. If you want one of the cabins around back, you have to pay extra. I'm not giving up mine. And you can't go through the snow in those shoes."

The woman glanced down at her cowboy boots, then back up

at me, unperturbed. "Honey, I don't know what you're talking about. I'm looking for Ethan."

I rolled my eyes. "All the gorgeous women are looking for Ethan. Get in line."

"No—I really am looking for him. It's urgent. Do you know where he is?"

I wasn't sure about her yet, so I hedged around the question. "We stay out of each other's way."

"Because of the fight in the airport," she supplied.

I scowled at her. "No, because he's a perfect asshole in a nice suit, and he's rubbed me the wrong way since birth. Whatever you want from him, you're probably not going to get it, but good luck."

"I'm his wife," the woman said.

I was stunned for a second, and then I laughed. "Sure."

"It's true. Want to see the marriage certificate?"

Oh, hell, this was sweet. Way too sweet to pass up.

"No, I don't want to see the marriage certificate." I motioned past her, where the crowd briefly parted to reveal Ethan behind the front desk, overwhelmed by the crowd and oblivious to what was coming. "But he probably does." I patted her on her sexy shoulder, which smelled like expensive perfume. "Welcome to the family."

I walked out the door, grinning to myself. However that little situation panned out, it had already made my day.

I WOULD RATHER BE KISSING Jasmine than signing autographs.

All told, signing autographs wasn't the worst part of my job. Mostly because a lot of the people standing in line were kids. I can be pissed off with most people, but who the hell can be pissed off with a kid who thinks you're a hero? Even I'm not that much of an asshole.

Still, the line was a long one and my hand was cramping. And I wasn't kissing Jasmine in this moment. I would rather be kissing Jasmine, feeling her soft lips melt against mine, hearing the little sound she made in the back of her throat. I'd spent seventeen years wishing I could kiss her again, and now that I'd had a taste of it, it was the only thing I wanted to do.

Well—not exactly the *only* thing. I had a list in my head. But I couldn't get to the list if I wasn't kissing her.

I nodded at the current autograph seeker and the next one stepped forward. This one was a girl of about eleven with red hair in a braid. She looked at me with wide eyes and handed me one of the NHL publicity photos Jasmine was handing out for people to sign. "My name's Alina," she said. "I play defense, like you."

"Yeah?" I took the photo and scrawled an autograph for her. "Left or right?"

"Usually right, but I can play either."

I nodded. The number of little girls in my lines got bigger each time, and it didn't surprise me. In a world with Hayley Wickenheiser, Serena Williams, and Megan Rapinoe, the women were creaming us in every sport. It was fun to see.

"My coach says I'm too small for defense," Alina said.

"Size isn't everything," I replied. "Show me your stick technique."

She mimed it, and I gave her pointers. I also gave her ideas for moves to practice so she would be more agile on the ice. "You gotta be fast," I told her. "You gotta show up before they know you're coming, because you already know where they're gonna aim. And you gotta be so fearless you scare the shit out of them."

Alina's mother looked sour at my language, but the little girl left elated.

I glanced past the line to where Jasmine was standing. We

were in the Salt Springs Arena, the rink I'd played on as a teenager before I got scouted. The ice was covered for the event, and I was at a table at one end. Next to me was a stand holding a large poster advertising the Kringle Inn and Christmas Tree Farm—*Open for the season! Your Salt Springs destination for Christmas joy!* I had no idea how Jas had gotten the poster made and printed so fast. She was a genius at this stuff.

She gave me a thumbs-up from her place by the line. She was wearing jeans today, the kind that skimmed her perfect body and showed off her flawless legs. I wished she would turn around so I could look at her ass. She had topped the jeans with a T-shirt that showed a green spring of mistletoe on a white background. The words on it were *Mistle My Toe.* I had no idea what that meant. I just knew I wanted the shirt off of her as soon as possible.

She noticed me staring at her and instead of getting mad, she blushed. I shook my writing wrist to signal her that I'd been here an hour and a half already. Jas bit her lip, counting the line, then mouthed the word *twelve.* I had twelve more autographs to go, and then I'd be done.

Then maybe we'd go to dinner.

My view of Jas was blocked by the next person in line—a woman. I looked around for the kid she was presumably with, but didn't see one.

"I'm so excited!" the woman said. She was about forty, wearing a knee-length dress with a jean jacket over it. Her dark hair was lushly styled and her makeup was perfect. She smiled right at me. "I'm such a big fan of yours!"

"Thanks," I said calmly, taking the photo from her hand. "Who should I make it out to?"

"Lisa. Can I get a selfie?"

Normally selfies were discouraged, partly for security reasons, mostly because they slowed down the line. But this signing was a special occasion, and Jasmine had declared that selfies were okay as long as they were quick. She wanted people posting their photos of the event on social media, which was part of getting the word out. Besides, most of the selfies were with kids.

Not this one. I pushed my chair back and stood as Lisa came around the table, phone in hand. She threw an arm around my neck as if we'd known each other forever and leaned so far in that I could smell her shampoo. She tapped the buttons on her phone, lining up the shot.

"Oh, God, you are *so hot*," she said breathily, and then, as she snapped the photo, she kissed me on the cheek, right above the line of my beard.

I grunted. *That* was definitely against the rules, but I stayed polite—I'd already ruined two of Jasmine's photo ops, and I wasn't going to ruin another one. I disentangled myself from Lisa, and as she walked away, I caught Jasmine giving me a death glare. Her smile was long gone. She looked like she could gladly commit murder.

Before I could say anything, she stepped in front of me to the head of the line. "Matt's time is almost up!" she shouted as the people still in line groaned in disappointment. "For those of you remaining, he'll only sign for kids! That's right, kids only! For the rest of you—sorry!"

She didn't sound sorry at all.

FOURTEEN

Jasmine

"THAT WAS ALMOST RUDE," Matt said. "Almost."

The autograph event was over—not a moment too soon. We were leaving the rink through the back doors, headed for my car. I was still fuming so hard I was seeing red.

"She *kissed* you!" I cried for the dozenth time. "Right in front of your fake girlfriend! The nerve!"

"It was on the cheek," Matt said.

I spun and looked at him. He had a smile at the corner of his mouth, which was Matt's version of hysterical laughter. He was wearing his dark wool coat and jeans, and he looked like a very, very large Abercrombie model. With a beard. And hockey thighs. And sort of a scowl. I wanted to jump him right here in the parking lot, which only made me madder.

I stomped up close to him, and he stopped walking. I peered at his face. "It's still there." I grabbed the Kleenex from my pocket and scrubbed the patch of skin where the woman had left a lipstick mark.

Matt winced. "You got it already, I think. The first ten times."

I didn't answer. That lipstick mark needed to be well and truly gone.

"You're jealous," Matt said.

I put the Kleenex back in my pocket. We were alone in the parking lot, the chilly December wind blowing around us. "No, I'm not."

"You are." He still sounded amused, damn him.

Of course I was jealous. It wasn't just the woman grabbing him and kissing him, though that had made me mad. Her lips should have been nowhere near him. But it was also what the entire incident represented.

Matt Kringle: Hot, hunky NHL legend with multimillion-dollar career and legions of women willing to sleep with him.

Me: Nobody PR girl, divorced former cheerleader, a couple of bad checks away from the unemployment line.

Just like that, my jealousy dissolved into pure, raw panic.

"Jasmine?" Matt must have read something in my face. He stepped close to me and cupped my face gently in his big hands, tilting me up to look at him. His dark eyes were serious. "This isn't about the kiss, is it? You look like you're freaking out." When I didn't speak, his expression changed as hurt flicked across his eyes. "This is the same expression you had when you broke up with me outside of the gym."

"We can't sleep together," I blurted. "I can't be your fake girl-friend. We can't be together. We don't work."

The words were out—wild, panicked, awful words. Just like that day seventeen years ago. But instead of looking like I'd punched him, Matt held his ground this time. His hands stayed on me. The only sign that the words had hit a mark was a twitch in his jaw.

"Yes, we can," he said, his gruff voice calm. "Yes, you can. Yes, we can. And yes, we do. If we want to."

I wanted to shake my head, tell him no, push him away. I wanted this to be over, no matter how much it hurt, because that would make the panic stop.

"It's impossible," I breathed.

"I'm a dumb kid from Salt Springs, Colorado," Matt said. "I won two Stanley Cups. Anything is possible."

"That's just it. You're—you. And I'm me."

His eyebrows rose. "A gorgeous woman with a great life and a fantastic career? Yes, you are."

I sighed. I still wanted to pull away, but my body wouldn't move. I liked the feel of him, the warmth of his hands too much. He'd put a spell on me. "Do you know why I broke up with you in high school?"

"No, I don't," Matt said bluntly. "I've always wondered. I've gone over and over it in my head, trying to remember if I did something wrong. Said something wrong. I can't come up with anything, but then again, my memory is faulty. The only thing I can seem to remember clearly is kissing you."

I made a strangled sound in my throat. Could you die by swooning? Just leave your earthly body and levitate?

"I knew this would happen," I said. "You becoming—you. Matt the Mountain, the legend. You always had the talent, Matt. Anyone could see it. You never did anything wrong—you did everything right. But you were going to leave and have this big life that didn't include me."

He frowned, listening to me intently. He was always good at listening instead of talking over me all the time.

"I couldn't handle it," I said, my pulse still hammering in my throat. "You going away forever to the NHL. With any other boy, it would have been fine. But with you, I knew it would hurt."

Matt seemed to follow my line of thinking. "So you broke up with me first," he said. "Before I could hurt you."

"I had to," I argued. He didn't understand, not really. I'd felt myself falling all those years ago. Hard. And that couldn't happen.

"Uh-huh," Matt said. "And you're doing it again."

"How would this work?" I asked him. "We have some fun for a few nights, and then you leave. Right? So long, see you in another seventeen years. Maybe."

He frowned, and he was quiet for so long that I got nervous. I reached up and tapped his forehead. "Hello?"

"Fuck," he said, and he kissed me. Just bent down and kissed me without a please or a thank-you, his mouth warm and insistent on mine. I put up not one iota of resistance. I put my arms around his waist and kissed him back, my body warm against his as the snowflakes swirled around us in the empty parking lot.

There was no one to see us this time, no one to take a picture. It was just us. We were doing this for just us.

Matt kissed me for a long time, and then he put his mouth to my neck, trailing kisses under my jaw and below my ear. His beard tickled my skin. I closed my eyes and shivered, melting against him.

"We would be so good," he said in a low voice, his breath against my skin.

Oh, God, we would. I was aching for him. I wanted to see everything, feel everything. I wanted to do all of the things we'd never gotten to do in high school. Except we'd be adults now, instead of a couple of fumbling kids—one of which, I knew for sure, had been a virgin at the time. That would be me.

The me of right now, who was a grown-ass woman, reached around Matt's waist, under his wool coat, and snaked my hands down the back of his jeans. I grabbed his gorgeous, hockey-player ass with both hands, gripping it just as I'd been longing to ever since he stepped off the plane. He made barely a twitch of surprise, and then he nibbled my earlobe, one big hand sliding down under my coat to cup my breast over my shirt.

I moaned and ducked my head, wanting him to kiss my mouth again. He did, his tongue tasting me expertly. We were a column of blazing heat in the December cold. And I replaced all of those old, teenage memories of making out with Matt Kringle with new ones. Hotter ones. Better ones.

He finally broke away from me, and I made a desperate sound. He ran a hand through his dark hair. "We haven't solved our problem," he said, his voice husky.

"Problem?" I had no idea what he was talking about. My own name was a blank.

Matt frowned. "You don't want a casual thing."

"Oh." Had I said that? Just minutes ago? What had I been thinking? I wanted him to do me right here in this parking lot. *Take me, sexy beast!* "Right. No, I don't. Because I have, um, self-respect."

Matt nodded. He was a little more clear-headed than I was, but not by much. "And I don't want a casual thing."

"You don't?" Wait, had he said that before? I was sure he hadn't.

"I don't," Matt reiterated.

"But—models," I said. "Pop stars. Women your height."

Matt shrugged, as if dating the most beautiful and talented women in the world was no big deal. "It isn't as fun as it sounds."

"I think Leonardo DiCaprio would disagree."

"Well, I'm not him. And whoever I dated isn't the point. The point is that I don't want something casual with *you*." He looked me up and down and sighed. "Fuck. I can't believe I just said that. I've been picturing you naked for seventeen years."

My mouth dropped open. "You have?"

"Of course I have," he grumbled. "And I just talked myself

out of seeing it, like an idiot. At this rate, I'll grow old and die before I see you naked."

"You should talk," I shot back. "I googled you yesterday, just in case you'd ever done one of those naked photo shoots. You know, the artsy ones they do of athletes sometimes where the leg is raised so no one sees the good parts. That's how desperate I am."

A smile touched the corner of his mouth. "I've been offered those kinds of shoots a lot of times. I've always said no."

"Believe me, I know you have."

"So we want to see each other naked," Matt said. "We've established that."

"We have."

"And yet we're not going to do it."

I crossed my arms, the chill of the winter air finally starting to cool me down. "I guess we aren't."

Our gazes locked.

"Fuck," Matt said, the word pure frustration.

I agreed.

FIFTEEN

Matt

MY BROTHER WAS DRUNK.

It was late, and Ethan was slouched on the chair in my cabin, his hair disheveled. He was wearing sweatpants and a mismatched zip-up hoodie. He had flip-flops on his feet, which he'd somehow worn through the snow to come and knock on my door.

My biggest mistake had been letting him in. Now he wouldn't shut up.

"Who does that?" he asked, his words slurring. "Who gets married in Vegas and doesn't remember it? I'm so fucked."

I sighed. Ethan didn't drink much—he was too goody-goody—but if he had been this drunk in Vegas, then I could see how the wedding thing had happened. According to his ramblings, the blonde I'd seen earlier really was his wife. Her name was Lexie, she was a Vegas showgirl, and he'd married her a year ago on a drunken weekend. Then he'd forgotten.

She'd come to the inn with divorce papers, expecting Ethan to sign them. Expecting that he'd be *overjoyed* to sign them. Instead, Ethan had hired her to work the front desk, which—it was fucking obvious to me, even if it wasn't to him—was a ploy to keep her around for a while. Because Ethan actually liked this woman who was apparently his wife. Normally, Ethan had no problem getting gorgeous women if he wanted them. The problem was that so far, Lexie had kept him in the friend zone.

I'd seen Lexie again, behind the front desk. She and Jasmine had hit it off, apparently agreeing that both of them were the boss of me. As a result, I was scheduled to skate on the pond regularly, to be seen by customers at the inn. The fact that this made me a zoo animal didn't bother either Lexie or Jasmine. The schedule had been written down and everything.

Still, Ethan was miserable. It would be funny, seeing my perfect big brother make such a colossal fuckup—if he would just stop talking. He had already said something about a sex tape, which made me want to gouge my ears out and throw up in my mouth at the same time.

"I wish I was drunk right now," I said.

"I mean, I barely remember her," Ethan rambled on. "I remember a little. There were shots. And she was really funny. And there was a bunch of sex. Incredible sex, to be honest." He blinked, remembering. "But I thought that was all it was. But it wasn't. And now she's here." He ran a hand through his already-messy hair, making it stand up. "I'm making a run for mayor, since Mayor Ethel is so old and retiring. But now I have *her*."

"I thought she was nice," I said.

"She *is* nice." As if he hadn't just implied the opposite.

I couldn't help needling him. "I also thought she was hot. I mean, come on. That body. Those curves. A smokeshow."

"A total smokeshow. But she doesn't fit in here. She doesn't fit in with my life."

"Do you want her to?"

"Not the point."

This was too easy. He really just needed to kiss the hell out of her, which I'd already told him. "If you don't want her, maybe I'll get her number. I need a date for the NHL Awards."

"Hey." Ethan gave me a blurry glare. "Stay away from her, hotshot. Just stay away."

I sighed, leaning back in my chair. I really did wish I was drunk. I was out of the habit during the season, and that hadn't changed, even now when I was benched. "In case you haven't noticed, I'm not much of a hotshot right now. Otherwise I'd be playing Tampa tonight instead of sitting here with you."

Ethan scrubbed a hand over his face. "It's really that bad?"

I gave a bitter laugh. My lower back ached just from sitting in this chair, as well as sitting for so long during today's autograph session. I needed to stretch it or it seized up. "It's that fucking bad," I admitted to my brother. I didn't talk about this with anyone, as if saying it out loud would make it more real. "It's my neck and my hip and everything else, but it isn't just the injuries. I'm not as fast as I was. My reflexes are slowing. They used the neck injury as an excuse for now, but the fact is that there are too many younger, faster guys coming up. They don't need me anymore, and I'm a liability. They're going to put me out to pasture."

"But you're the Mountain," Ethan said. Apparently alcohol brought out his loyalty. "The whole team revolves around you. You're a legend." He paused. "Or so I hear. You know, from other people."

"Right," I said. "Because you don't watch my games."

"I work long hours. I've seen them on TV in the occasional sports bar, I guess." He read my skeptical expression, then sighed. "Okay, busted. I watch when I can. And it's criminal that you aren't playing Tampa tonight. Their offense has been good all season. The Warriors need you, or they're going to lose."

"We're down two to one in the third," I said. "I may have looked. But Tampa doesn't matter. It's Minnesota we have to beat."

Ethan looked at me thoughtfully. "But you won't be playing Minnesota," he said.

"Considering my agent barely talks to me and the NHL has forgotten I exist, I don't think I will," I growled.

"Let me ask you something, little brother. Do you love hockey?"

When Ethan was being extra annoying, he called me *little brother*. Also, apparently, when he was drunk. "What are you, my therapist?" I barked at him.

"Just answer the question."

Fuck. I had reached my limit. I stood up and opened the minibar, taking out a tiny can of beer. It looked like a thimble in my hand.

I popped the top and drank it—not a very hard feat, since there were only a few tablespoons of beer in there.

"You're going to pay for that," Ethan couldn't help but point out. "It was probably twelve bucks. And you won't get a family discount."

"Fuck off," I said. "Yes, I like hockey. I think."

"You think?" Ethan's eyebrows rose. "And I didn't ask if you *like* it. I asked if you *love* it."

Love? I wasn't used to talking about love—not in any context. Not about sport, and definitely not about people. I put down the empty beer thimble and made a helpless gesture with my hands. "What the hell kind of question is that? Hockey is what I do. It's what I'm good at. Or, at least, what I used to be good at. It's what I was born for."

Ethan made a *tsk* sound. "You're still not answering the question."

"Do you love what you do?" I asked, turning the tables on him.

He shrugged. "I love what it represents. No one loves being a lawyer—but I think I might love being mayor. Doing good things for Salt Springs."

"You mean being in charge."

"I mean helping people. And yes, being in charge. But that's not the same as loving hockey."

"You can't love a sport," I argued. "It's a thing, not a person. It doesn't love you back."

"This is fascinating." Ethan pressed his palms together and placed his fingertips under his chin. "I'm just drunk enough to think this makes profound sense. Please don't disillusion me."

"Are you asking if I want to quit?" The thought made me want another thimble of beer, so I took one out of the mini fridge and opened it. "Fuck, I don't know." I downed a few more tablespoons of alcohol. "If I didn't play hockey, what would I do? Go work in a hardware store? Become an Uber driver? I have no social skills, no qualifications, and no fucking desire to do any of that."

"You could get married and have children," Ethan said.

I was so shocked I made a coughing sound. The first word that came to my mind was *Jasmine*. I pushed it away. "Here? In Salt Springs?"

"It's a nice place. You forget that I'm the only Kringle sibling who never moved away."

"I have a life in Chicago," I said, though even as the words came out of my mouth, they felt weird. I had an empty, soulless condo, a bunch of money, an empty schedule, and teammates. I didn't have close friends, a girlfriend, or even any hot, meaningless sex at the moment. I'd spent so many waking hours dedicated to hockey ever since I was a teenager that it had never crossed my mind to wonder what I would do if I wasn't playing.

"What if the Warriors drop you, or trade you?" Ethan asked me. "They might."

"Jeez, Ethan. Don't go easy on my feelings or anything."

"I'm your big brother. I'm supposed to tell you the truth." He pointed at me, and even though he was making sense, I could tell he was still drunk. Maybe that was the reason he was making sense. "You need to come up with a plan, little brother. The next act. Matt Kringle two-point-oh. Matt Kringle with upgraded RAM. The next chapter in the Matt Kringle saga—"

"I get it," I said.

"*The Empire Strikes Back,* but Matt Kringle." He nodded. "You're not at *Return of the Jedi* yet. But you're done with *A New Hope.*" He leaned back in his chair. "Hey, I have an idea. Want to watch *Star Wars?*"

SIXTEEN

Jasmine

WAS IT POSSIBLE, I wondered, that Kristen Kringle was cracking up?

No. It couldn't be.

Still, I looked more closely at her as we walked down a row of trees at the Christmas tree farm. When she'd first come to my apartment to interview me for the PR job, she'd been wearing a power suit and killer heels. Her hair and makeup had been perfect. But today, weeks later, she was wearing jeans, an oversized sweater, a mismatched parka, and a pair of boots that looked like they were 1) men's and 2) very old.

Sure, we were walking the rows of a Christmas tree farm in the snow, not sitting in an office, so of course Kristen wouldn't be wearing heels. But she also had no makeup on, her hair was coming out of its haphazard bun, and she was eating a doughnut. At two in the afternoon. A big, sugary doughnut with half an inch of pink icing on top. The entire thing looked like it weighed more than Kristen did.

Not that I was judging. I'd eat a doughnut like that any day of the week, and twice on Sundays. I just hadn't thought that Kristen Kringle ate them.

Maybe I was wrong.

"I'd offer you one of these," Kristen said, swallowing her bite, "but I only grabbed one. They were at the front desk, fresh from the bakery. You can get one if you want. Sorry. I just had a craving. My God, this thing is good."

"No problem," I said. The inn definitely had a lot of baked goods. Apparently, a baker had a contract to bring them every day. It was hard to resist them.

"Why haven't I eaten doughnuts all my life?" Kristen asked.

"Um, I don't know?"

"Me neither. When is the photo shoot you have planned with Matt?"

"In two hours." My heart gave a little jump at the thought of it, as did my lady parts. I had to tell them all to calm down. "We're doing it on the pond. We'll get some skating shots. Then I'll upload pictures to Matt's social media, tagging the inn and the farm." I'd already explained to her about Matt's millions of followers, who had never seen a single post from him.

"He's going to let you do that?" Kristen asked, glancing at me. "Like he actually said yes?"

Had he? It didn't matter—I would do it anyway. "Yes, he did."

"Wow." Kristen took another bite of doughnut. "You sure have a way with my brother. I've never been able to get him to do anything without twisting his nipple."

"I haven't had to do that," I agreed.

Kristen stopped walking abruptly, and I stopped before I bumped into her shoulder. "You see that?" she asked, pointing to a family that was picking out a Christmas tree. "And that?" She pointed to a couple that was doing the same thing. "That's what I call success. It's working—we have customers coming in. And they're leaving happy, despite the bad mood that *some people* have all the time. Don't you agree?"

"Um, yes. It's nice to see that—"

"Let's count my successes, shall we?" Kristen held up her fingers one at a time. "The inn has bookings. The tree farm has customers. We're planning a big Christmas Eve event. I turned things around. I am intelligent. I am confident. I get things *done.*"

She put the last bite of doughnut in her mouth. At the end of the aisle of trees, Paul, the manager of the tree farm, walked by. He was big and burly, with a dark beard. He was wearing plaid flannel and jeans. When he saw Kristen, he gave her a glare. She glared back. He kept walking.

"See what I mean?" Kristen said, her mouth full. "I should fire him." But her gaze stayed on Paul's back—or maybe his backside—as he walked away, as if she couldn't help it. And she sounded like she had no plans to fire him at all.

I cleared my throat, trying to get her attention. "So, about the Christmas Eve thing," I said. "It's only a few days away. The plans are coming together nicely."

"It's going to be great," Kristen said, tearing her gaze away from Paul's retreating form. "Music, hay rides, hot chocolate, that kind of thing. I've got most of it arranged. Matt could skate on the rink with the kids, if you can convince him. Everyone will come out and have a nice time." She licked sugar off her fingertip. "We should definitely have doughnuts."

I nodded. "I'll talk to Matt. I know a few local musicians if you still need some talent. I can get in touch with them for you." I smiled at her. "It must feel really good, knowing that you helped out your family like you have."

Kristen looked at me. "What?"

"You know, by turning this place around." I waved around me, indicating the Christmas tree customers. "You just said it yourself, it's a success. You've made a difference for the family business so it can prosper and carry on."

I thought it was a good speech, but Kristen just looked blank and sort of stricken. "Right," she said. "Prosper and carry on. Exactly."

I had no idea what I had said wrong. But I suddenly wished I had a doughnut.

I WAS SETTING up at the edge of the pond when Matt arrived, walking through the snow with a duffel bag over his shoulder. We were at the back of the Kringle property, behind the inn and the cabins, out of sight of the house and the tree farm. The pond had been flooded for Matt's skating and was frozen over, the smooth ice dusted with snow, and a cold wind blew across the surface. I felt it through the parka, hat, scarf, and mitts I wore. I was stomping my feet to keep the circulation going when I caught sight of him.

"You're not dressed," I said, taking in his jeans and wool coat, though at least he was carrying a hockey stick.

"You don't have a photographer," Matt said in reply. He looked me up and down. "And you look cold."

"I *am* the photographer." I gestured to the camera and tripod I was setting up. "I've done plenty of photography in my career. I can't do anything too advanced, but I can handle this."

"Uh-huh." Matt dropped the duffel bag, making the snow puff up around it. "And you're cold."

"Well, it's cold out. You're cold, too."

"I'm a warm person," he countered, coming closer. "I have a high natural body temperature. Or don't you remember?"

I did. Matt Kringle's big, hard body was like a natural furnace. Snuggling next to him was the best possible way to warm up when it was cold. I remembered it so clearly that for a second I wished I could unbutton his coat and climb inside. It would be so warm in there.

"Let's do this quick, before you become a popsicle." Matt unzipped the duffel bag. "I didn't know what you want me to wear. I found a pair of my hockey pants and a pair of my skates at my dad's house, but I don't have a Warriors jersey. I don't usually carry one around wherever I go."

"I brought one," I said, reaching into the bag I had brought, too. Luckily, when I bought the jerseys Kristen and Ethan had worn at the airport, I'd picked up a third one from the sports store. "It's the biggest size they carried. I hope it's big enough."

Matt took the jersey from me and shook it out. "It should work." He stared at the Warriors logo for a second, and something sad crossed his expression.

"Matt?" I asked him.

He shook his head. "Nothing. Just not sure how much longer I'll be wearing this. I called a few people this morning, looking for an update on the season. No one has called me back."

I swallowed. "Maybe it will work out," I said, though the thought of him flying back to Chicago, to his amazing NHL life complete with supermodels, made something squeeze in my chest. "Maybe they're just giving you time to fully recover, and then they'll put you back on the ice."

Matt dropped the jersey, then unbuttoned his coat and slid it off. He laid the coat on the snow and kicked his shoes off, standing in his socks on the coat. "You want to know the truth?" he asked. "I'm not even sure they should."

This was so surprising that I forgot how cold I was and I stared at him. Well, I also stared at him because he was stripping in front of me. "You don't want to go back? Don't you love hockey?"

"You sound like Ethan," he grumbled, his voice low and annoyed. He unbuckled his belt. "Why does everyone make me *think* so much?" He dropped his jeans and caught my expression as he stood there in his boxer briefs. "Relax, Jasmine. I'm not going to get naked. It's too cold for that out here, even for me."

"That's...fine," I said stupidly, staring at those amazing, muscled legs. Those boxer briefs.

Too quickly, Matt stepped into the hockey pants and pulled them up. "Don't look too closely," he warned me. "It's cold out here. It affects size."

Was he talking about—? Suddenly I wasn't nearly as cold. Actually, I felt a hot flush moving up my face and down through my body, to all the best spots. Size. Yes, a man as big as Matt would probably have a lot of girth. How much, though? Like, exactly how big was it? Really big?

While my brain was stuck in a loop, contemplating this, Matt quickly pulled the jersey on over his long-sleeved waffle shirt and dropped to the ground to lace on his skates. I tried to remember what we'd been discussing before I got distracted. "What did you mean when you said you aren't sure they should bring you back?"

He shrugged, his big fingers working quickly and gracefully on the laces. He must have done this thousands of times. "Just that I've taken a lot of hits in my career. I'm not young anymore. One of these days I'll take a hit that will be my last one. Maybe I should quit while I'm ahead."

I licked my lips, all thoughts of penis size forgotten. "Have you been hurt badly?" I asked.

He laughed without much humor. "It depends what you mean by badly. Everything has been broken, sprained, or strained at some point, most of it more than once. The groin was painful, but the neck injury really worried the doctors. I had to get tons of scans. Hairline fractures are tricky and hard to spot."

"A *fracture?*" He'd *broken his neck?* I almost felt faint at the thought. Why had I never thought about this?

"It wasn't a fracture," Matt explained. His voice was calm, as if it didn't concern him. "They just thought it was. They weren't sure at first. But I had to be careful in the off season. I'm not one of the team fighters, so I've only had two concussions in my career. But my lower back gets worse with every season. They could improve it with surgery, but then what? I go back out there one year older, and it gets injured again."

This was horrible. I knew hockey players got injured—of course I did. But I had never let myself think of Matt, the man I knew, getting a concussion or breaking his neck. Suffering in pain.

"You don't care that you could get hurt?" I asked him. "That doesn't scare you?"

He finished with his skates and stood, taking in the stricken expression on my face. "You're worried about me?" he asked, frowning.

"Of course I'm worried," I said. "Anything could happen when you play. Bad things. Terrible things."

He blinked, as if my answer surprised him. "Sure, it's a risk," he grunted. "It's what I signed up for. But at some point, you just have to do it. No one plays hockey forever. Everyone gets old."

"Matt, you're *thirty-four.*"

"Yeah." He scrubbed a hand through his thick, dark hair, his gaze moving to the ice. "Fuck, I hate thinking about this stuff. I'm gonna go skate. Let's get this over with. I did some stretches before I left the cabin, but give me a minute to warm up."

He moved with eerie grace on his skates to the edge of the pond, and then he sailed onto the ice as easily as if his big body weighed nothing. He started a circuit of the pond, his knees bending and his weight moving from side to side as he navigated the ice. I watched in awe as he circled once, getting a feel for what he was doing.

When he came back my way, he held out a hand. "Toss me the stick. You want some action shots?"

"Sure," I said, grabbing the hockey stick and reaching it out to him.

He grabbed it without slowing and did another circuit of the pond. This time I remembered to get behind my camera and adjust the shot through the viewfinder. As he skated past, I took shots, getting him in action, his jersey molded to his chest in the cold wind, his gaze focused like a laser, his body moving easily, the stick in his hands.

He did another circuit, and this time I shot it on video, getting Matt in motion with the sound of the wind and his skates scraping on the ice. We could post it on TikTok, though Matt probably didn't know what TikTok was. It was a quiet shot, meditative, beautiful. Just a man who was born to skate, doing it on a pond on a winter day, his body moving with effortless perfection. I wanted to watch Matt skate this pond for hours.

But it was really, really cold, and he was already doing me a favor, so I called out, "Let's do some still shots."

He skated back around toward me, his shoulders relaxing. His eyebrows rose. "Just me standing here?"

"Sure."

"You don't have any props for me or anything?" There was a hint of a smile on his lips. "No balloons? No models? No giant candy cane? No silly hat?"

"No," I replied. I hadn't had time to get any of those things, but now that we were here, props didn't seem right. All this shoot needed was Matt.

He stood facing the camera, the stick in front of him. Then with the stick in one hand at his side. Finally he posed with the stick on his shoulders, behind his neck, his hands holding it loosely. He put his weight on one hip, and my breath caught as I pressed the shutter, getting shot after shot.

He was the most beautiful man I'd ever seen.

He was my fake boyfriend.

He was going to leave town.

Suddenly, breaking up with him because I was scared of getting hurt seemed like complete stupidity. What was I thinking? I only had one life to live. There was only one Matt. I'd been without him for seventeen years because I was afraid. Wasn't that long enough?

Sure, it's a risk. But sometimes you just have to do it.

Didn't I deserve something really, really great for once? Something that was just for me?

I took my hands off the camera and realized they were shaking. Actually, all of me was shivering. I was freezing, and my throat was closing up as I tried not to panic and cry at the same time.

Matt frowned. "Jas?" he asked.

"Um." I tried to control my chattering teeth. "I think we're done."

"Oh, fuck. You're freezing." He skated to the pond's edge and walked toward me through the snow.

"I'm fine," I said.

"You're not. We've been out here too long. Pack up your camera. We're going." His voice was rough. He bent and unlaced his skates.

I made my fingers work as I took the camera off the tripod and packed it in my bag. "I just need some—some hot chocolate," I said. "It will warm me—warm me right up."

Matt slid his feet into his boots and picked up his coat from the snow. "My cabin is just over there."

Part of me was still panicking. "I can—I can just go home. It's no big deal."

"Absolutely the fuck not." Matt picked up my bag along with his, then steered me through the snow. "We're going to my cabin. Now."

SEVENTEEN

Matt

I WASN'T TRYING to make a move when I brought her to the cabin. Honestly, I wasn't. Okay, sure—I'd invited her to my cabin before. A guy has to try, especially with a woman like Jasmine.

But she'd said no to my come-on, and then she'd said that she didn't want a one-time thing, that she wanted to keep it professional, even though we were fake dating. So, fine. I got that message loud and clear.

Fuck, I did *not* want to be professional.

She unzipped her parka when we got inside the cabin. Thank God I'd turned the heat up, and it was nice and warm. I'd never seen Jasmine shake with cold before.

I took her coat and looked more closely at her face, and I realized she was freaking out. Again.

"What did I do?" I asked her, because I honestly had no idea. I'd put on a jersey and skated around the pond a few times, just like she'd asked me to. Why was she freaking out?

"Nothing," she said, her voice quavering. "I'm just cold."

I wasn't going to get it out of her, so I took off my own coat. "Take off your boots," I told her. "We'll get under the blankets."

"We?" she asked, though she unzipped her knee-high boots to take them off.

"Yes. I'm warm, remember?"

I also wanted to get her under the blankets. Maybe if I could get my arms around her, I could get a better idea of what was wrong.

I took off my boots and pulled the Warriors jersey off over my head, leaving me in hockey pants and a long-sleeved waffle shirt. I grabbed the extra blanket folded at the foot of the bed and shook it out. Then I pulled the covers back. "Get in," I said to Jasmine.

She got in, fully clothed in jeans and a red zip-up hoodie that hugged her curves. She lay on her side, her knees pulled up, and I got in behind her, spooning her. I pulled the blankets up over us and put my arms around her, squeezing her into my chest.

I heard her sigh, and her body relaxed into mine. She was still shivering. I squeezed her tighter.

"This would work better naked, you know," I said.

"Matt."

"I know. Nothing casual. I know."

She sniffed. She really was cold, the chill seeping out of her as I held her. Her ass fit neatly against me and her hair smelled nice. I was in bed with Jasmine, and for a minute I was simply happy about it. Simply happy, period.

I was happier in this bed, in this cabin, than I'd been playing hockey for a while.

"Should we talk about something?" I asked her.

"About how embarrassing this is?" she offered.

"It isn't embarrassing." I rubbed a hand over her arm. "I've been wondering. How the hell did you end up marrying Gareth Green?"

"Oh." Jasmine groaned, putting her hands over her eyes. "Now, *that* is embarrassing."

"Tell me," I said. "I just froze my balls off, skating around the ice so you could get a photo. So you have to tell me."

"Ugh." She groaned again, as if it was painful. I tried not to smile. "Okay, well. He asked me out after we broke up—"

"After *you* broke up with *me*," I interrupted.

"Fine. After I was very, very stupid and broke up with you. Are you satisfied?"

"A little."

She was starting to warm up now, and she settled back, getting even closer. Her ass wiggled against me. "We dated. Then high school ended, and we just kind of kept going. Everyone expected us to be together by then, you know? Everyone thought we matched."

I did not like this story. Not at all. But I stayed quiet.

"So the next thing I knew, we'd been dating for two years, and everyone was asking when we were getting married. My family, his family, all of our friends—everyone expected it. So Gareth proposed, and everyone expected a big wedding. So we planned a big wedding. It took a year and a half."

"What?" I grunted, certain I had heard wrong. "Planning a wedding took a year and a half?"

"Oh my God, yes. The venue, and the dress, and the brides-maid's dresses. The flowers and the meal. The music. I did almost nothing else for eighteen months. I had my PR diploma by then, but I was so busy I didn't work much. Gareth got a job selling real estate. We got a place together. And that was *before* everyone started bugging us to have babies."

"I hate this story," I admitted.

"I didn't have babies with Gareth," Jas said. "I can say that much for myself. But everyone expected me to. No one expected me to do anything else."

"Right. So you had a wedding."

"Finally, yes. The big day came. I had the dress and the bridesmaids and everything. My mother cried; Gareth's mother cried. It went off perfectly. And after it was over, at the end of the day, I had this crazy thought: Without the wedding to plan, I had no idea what I was supposed to do with this man. Or with myself. Or my life. It was like the wedding was the point, not the actual marriage." She took a breath. "It was a completely terrifying thought, so I tried not to think it. I tried through the honeymoon and afterward. Within months, we were being pressured to get pregnant. And I wanted to scream, *I don't even want to be married! I haven't gotten over that part yet!*"

"Jesus, Jasmine," I said softly. "What about work?"

"I wanted to work," she said. "I love what I do. I wanted to build my career. But Gareth thought my job was just fluff, an excuse for me to wear nice clothes and makeup. Everyone thought that as soon as I had a baby I would quit." She was all the way against me now, our bodies locked together and warm. "I didn't know what to do. I'd worked so hard on the wedding, it seemed crazy to give up on the marriage. I thought I should make a go of it. Then Gareth cheated with one of his coworkers, and it all blew up."

"I saw your posts on Facebook," I admitted. "You weren't married very long."

"Fourteen months," Jasmine said. "I spent longer planning the wedding than I did as a wife. Isn't that pathetic?"

"Not at all," I said. "At least you got out. You built your career, just like you wanted to. Fuck that guy."

"I did build my career," she said. "And then the scabies chef happened, and the dog walking thing, and the fire."

"So what? Now you have the job here. You just rebuild. Aren't you the one who told me I'm not old yet?"

Jasmine rolled partway onto her back, looking up at me. Her

blond hair was spread over the pillow. She smiled. "Matt Kringle. Are you giving me a pep talk?"

Was I? Shit. "Was it any good?"

"Pretty good."

We smiled at each other. She was so beautiful. I wanted to kiss her. All I had to do was lean down and—

Jas bit her lip and panic flashed in her eyes. She put her palms on my chest, a signal that I shouldn't get any closer. I froze.

"I forgot," she said, her voice high and tense. "Let's check the photos and post some of them to Instagram."

"Jasmine," I said, but she was already pushing away from me, sliding off the bed and rifling through her camera bag. "We can pick a photo and I can send it to your phone," she said briskly. "Then we can post it. Let me do the post, if you don't mind. I know how to use hashtags."

I sighed and flopped back on the bed, running my hands through my hair. I was sexually frustrated, but I was also confused. I had been so close to getting Jasmine to break through whatever was holding her back. Why was this girl so terrified?

And why did I want her to give in so bad? It wasn't just a one-time thing, not for me. Why did I want Jasmine, when my life was in Chicago?

My life doesn't have to be in Chicago.

The thought hit me as I stared at the ceiling. Beside me, sitting on the edge of the bed, Jasmine had picked up her phone. She had tapped on something and was reading, scrolling through a page.

"Oh," she said.

My thoughts still spinning, I turned my head and looked at her. Whatever she was reading had made her cheeks go a shade of red that matched her hoodie. Her hair was tousled from lying in bed with me, and I wanted to kiss her so bad it was an ache all over my body. "What is it?" I asked her.

"Someone tweeted me the statement you put out. About the candy cane thing." She scrolled to the top and read it again. "I can't—is this for real? Did you really put this statement out?"

I frowned. "It better be right. Someone's head will roll if it isn't. I double-checked it myself before it went out."

Jasmine read from the statement. "The woman in the photo is not an employee. Her name is Jasmine Collingwood, and she is one of the most experienced, sought-after PR professionals in the state, who has graciously agreed to a contract with the Kringle family at the expense of her busy schedule. Jasmine was also my girlfriend in high school, and since I have come back to Colorado, I have been lucky enough to win her back. We have known each other for seventeen years, and I most certainly was not harassing her. This photo is a quiet moment between me and the woman who knows me better than anyone. Please respect our privacy and leave us alone."

I scratched my beard, pleased. "Okay, good. They got it right."

"You *said* this?" She turned her phone screen to me, as if I could read it. "You said I'm an experienced and sought-after PR professional? I have twelve new emails in my inbox."

"Good," I grunted. "You've worked hard to promote my family business. I thought it was time I promoted you for once."

"You said..." Jasmine paused. She blinked, as if she was close to tears. "You said you're lucky to win me back. You said I know you better than anyone. You said all of those sweet things." A sigh whooshed out of her, and she wiped under her eyes. "Oh. Oh, my God."

"I meant it," I said. I didn't like that she was crying. Women crying was my nightmare. "I know the dating is fake, but I still meant that part. You know it's true."

She put the phone down on the bed and pressed her hands to her eyes. She took a deep, hitching breath.

"Please don't cry," I said. "It's just a statement. I can put out a correction if you want."

"A *correction?*" She let out a sobbing laugh. "Don't you dare. I know I'm being weird. I just..." She took a deep breath and dropped her hands. "I feel a lot for you, too. I felt it in high school, and I feel it now. And my feelings are terrifying."

I didn't say anything. My heart had started pounding in my chest. The only woman who made my heart pound like this was Jasmine.

"Everyone told me what I was supposed to want," Jasmine said. "And I didn't want any of those things. I spent a long time figuring out what I *do* want. It's worth it, going against the script that everyone has for me, but it's also really, really hard. Most of the time I feel like no one believes in me. Especially lately." A tear trickled down her cheek. "And then you say all of *this*. And it's terrifying. But Matt..."

She stopped, and I couldn't take it. My heart was in my throat. "What? Just say it, Jasmine. Just say it."

But she didn't say it. What she did instead was crawl across the bed, straddle me, lean down, and kiss me.

My hands immediately went into her hair as I kissed her back. She tasted good, and her hair was like silk against my fingers. She felt very good sitting on my lap, and the longer we kissed, the more I felt myself get hard.

Damn it. I wanted this, but I hadn't put out that statement so that I would get laid. I broke the kiss and looked into Jasmine's eyes. "If you don't want to do this, we need to stop now," I said.

Her response was to pull back, unzip her hoodie, and toss it away. She was wearing a white tank top underneath. She took that off and tossed it, too, leaving her in a nude-colored bra. A second later, that was gone.

"Okay," I said, my voice a croak as I stared at her.

Jasmine saw the look in my eyes and smiled. She lifted her

arms, bending her elbows so that her hands were behind her head in a seductive pose that made her breasts lift. They were peach-sized and perfect, made to fit in my palms. I raised my hands to touch her, but she pushed off me and stood next to the bed.

I was alarmed until I realized that she was taking off her socks, then unbuttoning her jeans. She hooked her thumbs in the waistband, then looked at me, her gaze playful and sexy at the same time.

"You said you wanted to see me naked?" she asked.

Was this really happening? After all this time? I made my voice work before I lost my chance. "Hell yes, I do."

"Good," Jasmine said, and she dropped the last of her clothes to the floor.

EIGHTEEN

Jasmine

I WASN'T sure who this woman was, this version of Jasmine who stripped naked in front of Matt Kringle. This Jasmine was a confident seductress who saw what she wanted and went for it, risk be damned.

Then again, maybe I *did* recognize her. She was the seventeen-year-old version of me who had told Matt Kringle to ask her out in English class.

Matt didn't speak when I kicked off the last of my clothes. He made a choked sound in the back of his throat that was very gratifying, and then he swung his legs over the edge of the bed, sitting up. He put his hands on my hips and pulled me toward him. I came, straddling his lap as he pulled me onto him, bracing myself with my hands on his shoulders.

He kissed me, a devouring kiss that made me dizzy. His beard scraped my skin and his hands moved up my bare back, his palms hot on my skin. I felt the fabric of his pants against my inner thighs, the knit of his shirt against my nipples, the heat of his body through the layers, and even though Matt was fully clothed, the sensation made tingles rush through my body. I melted against him.

His hands moved down my back again, so warm and capable, and as his tongue tangled with mine, he cupped my ass and pressed me against him. I gasped against his mouth.

"Too much?" he asked.

"Get naked," I replied, my voice a whisper. Then I added, "Please."

Matt smiled. He smiled like this so rarely, a true smile that lit up his face, and for a second I lost my breath at how unbearably handsome he was. A beard and a scowl could never disguise the real Matt—not to me. To me, he was the most gorgeous man in the universe.

He lifted me gently off his lap, then pulled off his shirt in that stupidly sexy move men do where they reach behind their neck. I wanted to watch him do that a thousand times. Then I lost all thought as I saw his bare chest. He'd taken his shirt off during a few of our teenaged makeout sessions, but now he had a man's chest, an athlete's chest, broad and muscled and dusted with dark hair. I wanted to run my fingers over it, but he wasn't done.

He put his hands to the waistband of his pants. I was going to see the glory of Matt Kringle in all of his naked perfection, a reward for every good thing I'd ever done in life—and then he stopped.

Matt frowned. "Hold on."

There was the distinct sound of an old-school record scratching in my head as I stood there, naked. "*Hold on?*" I practically shouted at him. "*Hold on?*"

"You don't carry condoms on you, do you?"

I glanced down at my buck-naked body. "Do I look like I have a condom somewhere?"

"Wait. I might have one." His gaze caught on me. "Don't move. Give me one second. I'll beg if I have to, Jasmine. Just don't move."

I huffed out a breath and put my hands on my hips. Matt nearly leapt off the bed, going for his duffel bag on the floor. I heard him rifling through it, then cursing.

"Matt," I warned.

"Wait," he growled. "One minute. Wait." More shuffling. "Fuck." Something thumped. "Okay, crisis averted. I have condoms."

Condoms? As in more than one? Now I was wondering why Matt traveled around with entire packs of condoms at the ready. It wasn't a pleasant thought, especially in this very naked moment.

He came back in front of me with a strip of condoms in his hand. I caught a glimpse of familiar navy-and-green colors, and my eyes went wide. "Where did you get those?"

"The team gives them out," Matt said, tossing the strip in the bed. "We all get them."

"The team gives out condoms with the Chicago Warriors logo on them?"

He shrugged. "I guess they figure, better safe than sorry. And if you're going to equip your team with condoms, you may as well make them team condoms." He put his hands on my hips, and now he was touching me again and I was up close with that gorgeous, bare chest. "I carry them because the team tells me to, Jasmine. Relax."

I ran my tongue over my lip. I had the sudden, crazy urge to tell him to forget the condoms—I was clean, and he probably was, too. Then I remembered that I wasn't on the pill anymore, because my dating life was so sad that I hadn't needed any birth control. And where had that thought come from, anyway?

Matt tilted my face up to his, then gently tapped my forehead with a fingertip. "Hello," he said.

I blinked at him, because I was recalling where I was in my cycle, and now I had the thought in my head that I could get pregnant. Right now. With Matt.

And that sounded kind of...awesome?

Which was insane. We hadn't even had sex yet. We weren't a thing. He'd probably run screaming from the room if I said it out loud.

I was finally, *finally* about to have sex—most likely great sex—with Matt Kringle, and I was going to ruin it.

Just no.

"Hi," I said back to him, pushing the thought away. I put my hands on his bare chest, feeling the soft hairs under my palms. I ran my fingers down to his stomach, which was hard as a rock, and I practically forgot my own name.

A sigh of breath left him, and I realized I'd worried him for a minute. He lowered his mouth to mine and kissed me, and we were off to the races again.

We both pulled off his pants and boxer briefs, and a minute later he was completely naked, pulling me back toward the bed, still kissing me. He got back on the bed and pulled me onto his big, hard, bare body.

"I don't want to crush you," he said. "Get on top."

Oh, I definitely wanted him to crush me. That sounded delicious. But I got on top of him, and instead of feeling his clothes this time, I felt his skin. Everywhere. Between my thighs, against my hands, against my body as I leaned onto him in a deep kiss. Just the warm feel and delicious smell of Matt, all of him, under me and on me and all around, all of him mine.

His hand slid down between us, and then his fingers were working magic, and I was rocking on him, helpless as the pleasure built and built. I'd always wanted Matt to touch me there, and we were just getting started. I closed my eyes and let myself go, relaxing into how good he made me feel.

It didn't take long before I came, my hips rocking as I gasped. Matt swore in a low growl, his voice tight. Then he grabbed one of the condoms, slid it on, and put his hands on my hips, moving me. A second later I slid down over him.

"Oh, fuck, Jasmine," he said.

I was suddenly insatiable. I had never felt like this before. I took him deep and rocked on him again, letting my body move by instinct. Matt was propped up on one elbow, his other hand on my hip, guiding me as I moved. His eyes were dark, his body rigid. I put my hands on his chest and changed the angle of my hips, and his fingers dug harder into my hips. I got to watch as he came undone, his head tilting back and his hips lifting powerfully under me as he came. It was spectacular. I wanted to see it again and again. A hundred times.

We crashed to the bed on our backs, both of us breathing hard. I was sore and incredibly happy. Matt had a trickle of sweat running down his neck to his collarbone.

We were quiet for a minute, the easy quiet of two people enjoying the moment. I broke the silence.

"So that's what great sex feels like," I said to the ceiling.

"No," Matt said. "That's what *incredible* sex feels like."

I felt myself smiling. And I knew he was, too.

NINETEEN

Matt

"THIS IS STUPID," my dad said.

I gripped the steering wheel of my rental car and drove through the snow of downtown Salt Springs. Silently, I agreed with him. I was driving my dad to a doctor's appointment, and I was doing it because of my own idiocy.

When I had met Paul McCleer that first day—that Paul Bunyan do-gooder interloper—I had opened my big mouth and asserted that he didn't need to take Dad to doctor's appointments, because I could do it. That's right, me. The NHL player who was only in town for a few days.

Now I had to put my money where my mouth was. Dad was going to a checkup, and out of pride and a need to beat McCleer, I insisted on driving him. So far, neither of us was happy with the situation.

"Paul could have done this," Dad complained.

"The hell he could," I said. "You already have a son. Two of them, actually. We don't need that guy."

Dad frowned at me. He had put a red knit cap on over his white hair, and it made him look like a Santa Claus who had done a good amount of weed in the early eighties. "You always were a stubborn ass."

"I wonder where I got that trait from."

Dad snorted. "Not from your mother, that's for sure."

We both went quiet. We never talked about it, but we both missed Mom. She'd been gone for three years now, and it hadn't gotten any easier.

I made a turn. "This is looking to be a good Christmas season," I said, trying to make conversation.

"No thanks to me," Dad said. "First Rhonda behind the front desk quit, so Ethan hired some girl named Tammi. With an I."

"Tiffani with an I," I corrected him.

"Whatever. He didn't even ask me. Then, after I broke my leg, your sister showed up and started going through the books. Talking about how we don't have enough bookings. Like I care about bookings! This is my family business, not some big New York corporation with shareholders. Your mother and I started it decades ago as a labor of love. With her gone and all of you moved on to your lives, what am I doing it for?"

My throat closed. I didn't like to think about Dad all alone with Mom gone, not bothering with the business anymore. "I think Kristen is just worried about your retirement," I said.

"I have plenty," Dad said. "How much does one man need to live on? A roof over my head and a little food, that's all I need. The inn and farm make enough to pay my bills, and I don't care about more than that. The only change I actually like is Paul, because he cares about the trees and the environment. It isn't all about money with him. I like that boy."

Paul again. I needed to kick that guy's ass. I wondered if Dad would like him so much if he knew that Paul might be banging his daughter, something I suspected every time I saw the two of them together. What was it with my siblings and their sex lives? I needed a lifetime supply of eye bleach.

Dad was on a roll now, and I couldn't get a word in, even if I bothered to try. "I have a broken leg, you know. I'm not dead. I can still do things. But you wouldn't know it, going by your brother and your sister. They won't let me do a damn thing."

"I know the feeling," I said, finding a spot and maneuvering to park the car. "The NHL treats me the same way. A guy has a groin pull and he maybe breaks his neck once, and suddenly he's useless."

"Screw those guys," Dad said.

I blinked at him. "The NHL? Screw the NHL?"

Dad gave me a level look. "What do you owe them? They got your best years, health-wise. You don't owe them everything else you want to live for."

I stared at him, shocked. Ever since I was a kid with talent, I'd been told that the NHL was the ultimate goal. The best possible thing I could do with my life. I'd been told by teachers, coaches, my friends, fellow players, even my siblings. But —not Dad.

Dad had never told me that my only worth was in making the NHL. Not once.

"Aren't I supposed to love hockey?" I asked him.

"What the hell are you asking me for?" Dad shot back. "Do you love hockey or don't you? It seems like a question you should be able to answer. You're what, thirty-four? Jeez. All I'm saying is that even if you love hockey, you don't have to do what a bunch of corporate suits tell you to do. Your mother and I didn't raise you that way. If you want to do something else, then screw everyone and do it."

I finished parking and turned the car off, staring out the

windshield for a second. What an idiot I was. What a complete and utter idiot.

Every time a problem came up at home—the inn not doing well, Dad breaking his leg—my answer had been to throw money at it. Like an asshole. Because it was easier than actually dealing with things, especially after Mom died. If I threw money at things, I could feel like I was solving them without actually solving them.

Dad hadn't raised me that way. Neither had Mom. Which meant I didn't have to do that anymore. If I wanted to, I could do things differently. I could do whatever I wanted.

I looked at the office building that housed Dad's doctor's office. It had steps up the front, and they were covered with icy snow.

"Well?" Dad asked, impatient. "Are we getting out of this car, or are we going to sit here all day?"

"You can't get up those steps in crutches," I said.

"The hell I can't."

"Not alone." I opened my door. "Get out, old man. We're going up together."

"I can do it," Dad grumbled, but he had to maneuver his crutches out of the car, and he insisted on doing it before I could circle around to help him, and he almost fell over. There was no way he could do steps in this snow. If he broke his neck, I would never forgive him.

I took the crutches in one hand. "Put your arms around my neck."

Dad complained at top volume, but he did it. Deep down, he didn't want to break his neck, either.

I hefted him up against my side, lifting him off the ground. Except for the cast, he didn't weigh very much. I lifted him up one step, then another.

"This is just great," I grunted. "Someone's gonna take a

picture, I can feel it. I've already been on the internet for groping Jasmine. Now I'm gonna be on the internet for abducting an old man."

Obligingly, Dad turned his head and shouted for the benefit of the passers-by. "This is Matt Kringle, and he's not abducting me! He is my son! I am participating of my own free will!"

I hefted him up another step, and another. Just a guy helping his dad in the snow. It was stupid and completely absurd.

So why did I feel like crying, and like laughing at the same time?

TWENTY

Jasmine

"HERE'S THE THING ABOUT MEN," Lexie said, picking up a chocolate chip cookie. "They're...well, men."

I bit into a ginger snap, listening raptly. Kristen looked skeptical, but I noticed she was listening too, a brownie in her hand. "That's it?" she asked. "Men are men? That's your wisdom?"

We were sitting in Kristen's small office at the inn. The front desk had just closed for the evening, which meant Lexie was off work. She'd taken over the front desk the day she showed up to get a divorce from Ethan. Because she was, apparently, Ethan's wife.

That story was juicy. I couldn't picture hot, buttoned-up Ethan letting loose in Vegas and getting drunk-married, but apparently it had happened. I liked Lexie a lot—she was friendly and fun to be around. She was also gorgeous.

Kristen was a successful CEO, but Lexie had different skills. Like, she knew how to wear sequins without looking ridiculous.

And leather pants! If I wore leather pants, I would be laughed out of Salt Springs. Yet I was sure that if Lexie wore them—and she undoubtedly owned a pair—everyone would just drool.

"You know what I mean," Lexie said, crossing her amazing legs. "Men are oblivious, and forgetful, and self-absorbed." She sighed. "They can also be wonderful. Which is the entire problem."

I nodded. Lexie knew a lot more about men than I did—and more than Kristen did, I suspected. She'd seen it all. I definitely... hadn't. So I needed advice.

Things were going great with Matt—really great. After our session in his cabin, we'd talked for a long time. Then we'd had a shower, which led to other things. Then we'd gone back to the bed again.

Athletes, it turned out, had a lot of endurance. Like, a *lot*.

Still, I needed guidance. What, exactly, were Matt and I doing? Was I supposed to ask him where this was going? He was going to leave for Chicago again. Was I supposed to be mad about that, or supportive? Were we supposed to talk about it? Because if Matt had his way, we definitely wouldn't talk about it. If Matt had his way, every time I brought it up, he'd kiss me until I forgot what I was saying.

Which was wrong, but also so amazing that I was all in, every time.

Hence, here I was, sitting in this office, hoping for advice. And eating baked goods. Kristen was here, too, so she must want advice about something—probably to do with Paul McCleer, the hottie who ran the Christmas tree farm. I'd seen her stare at his backside. There was definitely something going on.

"My first question," Lexie said, looking at Kristen and me. "Before I can give advice, I have to know. Is the sex good?" She took in our shocked expressions. "Please, don't pretend it isn't happening, either of you. I can tell."

"I don't know what you're talking about," Kristen said, punctuating the sentence with a huge bite of brownie.

I was a horrible liar, so I just cleared my throat and wished a hole would open up under my feet. "Yes."

"Well, that's something," Lexie said.

"Here's my question." I leaned forward, my ginger snap temporarily forgotten. "I've been divorced for ten years. What if I want babies? Not tomorrow, but someday? Do I bring that up?"

"You can't lie about that," Lexie said. "If it's something you want, especially with him, then you have to tell him."

"But I don't even know if we're a thing. We've been fake dating, except that we're really dating. Except that he'll go back to his life in the NHL any day now."

"Do airplanes exist?" Lexie asked. "Does Matt Kringle have all the money in the world? Then it's fine. He can fly here and impregnate you anytime he feels like it." She looked me up and down. "Frankly, he could have done it anytime since the divorce, if both of you weren't so stubborn. But that's just my opinion."

"Easy for you to say," Kristen said. "You're already married to Ethan, and you don't have a high-powered career to go back to." She held up a hand. "You're really good at your job, Lexie. Like, the best. I know that. But how much financial security does it give you? And can you do it past forty?"

It was a hard truth, but it was the truth. Lexie couldn't grow old as a Vegas showgirl. She could, however, have a great life as Ethan's wife here in Salt Springs. I wished she would stay, because it would be awesome to be friends with her. But it was none of my business.

"I worked hard to get out of Salt Springs," Kristen went on. "I spent years building a great career. I can't just dump that to move home. If I can land another job in New York, I have to take it."

If I can land another job? What did that mean? Lexie and I exchanged a look, and I silently shrugged my shoulders. I thought Kristen *had* a job.

But she seemingly hadn't noticed her slip. "I have to be practical," she was saying. "I have to be logical. I can't just throw caution to the wind and let him have my mug."

Lexie and I looked at each other again. "I'm not sure I can help you with that one," Lexie said. "Sometimes you just have to follow your heart. That goes for both of you."

"My heart definitely does not know what it's doing," Kristen said.

"Mine isn't the brightest," I added. "Like, it doesn't always read the *push* or *pull* signs on doors."

"I get that," Lexie said. "But your heart is probably smarter than you give it credit for."

I looked at her. "What about your heart?"

Lexie sighed, looking troubled, and I knew she was thinking about Ethan. She picked up another cookie and bit into it.

"My heart wants a martini," she admitted. "Actually, lots of them. And make them all doubles."

I KNOCKED on the door of Matt's cabin. "It's me."

"Come in," he said.

He was sitting on the bed, his back against the headboard, a laptop in his lap. He was wearing nothing but boxer briefs, and he was frowning at the screen. He glanced up at me. "Hey," he rumbled. "You missed my skate. Where have you been?"

"Eating cookies with Lexie and Kristen."

"That's nice." He looked at the screen again.

"What are you looking at?" I asked him, unzipping my coat and dropping it on a chair.

"Stats," Matt said, and he sounded extra grumpy about it. "The Warriors are in a good position to make the Playoffs."

"Oh." I paused, looking at his scowl. "That's good, right?"

"Yeah, it's good." He ran a hand over his beard. "Even though they're going without me, the fuckers. I'm worried they're going to trade Wellerman. All signs point to it, but it would be a stupid move. I hope they don't do it."

I felt a rush of happiness, looking at him, even as grumpy as he was. Matt wanted what was best for his team, whether he was playing or not. He was that kind of guy.

Oblivious, forgetful, and self-absorbed, Lexie had said.

"Matt," I said, "When is my birthday?"

"May eleventh," he replied, without looking up from his laptop. "You wanted a makeup kit for your seventeenth birthday, but your parents gave you a thousand-piece puzzle instead. You said it was the worst birthday present you ever got."

My toes curled and my heart jumped, and for the first time I thought maybe I was in love with Matt Kringle. "What was my favorite music in high school?"

"That country singer," he said without missing a beat. "The hot one from the nineties. What's her name—Shania Twain. You liked to play her music in the car and sing along." He looked up. "Why are you asking me these things?"

I could barely breathe, looking at him. "You got the answers right."

"Of course I did." He closed the laptop and set it aside. "Come here."

I did. I took off my shoes and got in bed with him, and the next thing I knew, Matt Kringle was kissing me. Then he unbuttoned my shirt and tugged down my bra and his mouth was on my nipple, hot and insistent. I felt it in every nerve in my body.

We were supposed to talk. It was probably important. But I reached into his boxer briefs and wrapped my hand around his hard cock, and he moaned into my neck like it was the best thing he'd ever felt. He undid my jeans and slid them down, along with my underwear, kissing me deeply the whole time. I kept my hand on him because I liked the feel of him so much. Because I craved every inch of him.

He was big, and he was perfect, and in this moment he was all mine. I didn't want to talk anymore.

"We're going to need another team condom," I said against his mouth.

"I still have a few left." He pushed me onto my back, moving over me. "Do I weigh too much? Tell me if it doesn't feel good."

He was pressing me into the bed, all of him perfect on top of me. "It feels good," I said, telling him the truth. I wrapped my legs around his hips, and he moaned again.

He grabbed a condom, and then he was pressing into me, big and delicious. I was overwhelmed in the best way, with the size of him, his scent, the heat from his big body, the careful way he moved to make sure I got pleasure from every stroke.

I wanted this to be my life. I wanted it to last forever. I wanted everything.

TWENTY-ONE

Matt

"MATT KRINGLE," said Chet Brett, the sports radio host. "So great to have you here, man. I have a ton of questions."

I nodded. We were in the studio of a sports radio station in Denver, where Chet was the host of *NHL Daily*. Then I remembered that it was radio and no one could see me, so I said, "Nice to be here."

"Cool, man, cool," Chet said. He had long, graying brown hair in a ponytail and a matching graying brown beard. "You're one of the greats, man. I remember that game seven five years ago. Just incredible, all the way into double overtime. I've never seen anything like it. I was amazed you were still standing by the end."

I remembered Jasmine's advice for this interview, which she'd written down on a piece of paper in her distinctive, girly handwriting. *Be personable! Be charming! Be you!* I had the paper in my pocket. "That game was pretty grueling," I said, trying to sound natural. "I won't lie. But it was worth it for the Cup in the end."

"For sure!" Chet gave me a thumbs-up. I didn't know whether that meant I was doing well, or whether he just did that all the time. "I get this season has been rough. You're here in Colorado to see family for the holidays while the team is playing. That has to be hard."

"It hasn't been so bad," I admitted. "It's been good to see my family. We have a family business, an inn and Christmas tree farm, and I've been so busy that I haven't had time to get involved. But this year, I've been able to help out my family, especially my dad. It means a lot."

There. I had slid in the mention of the business, which was why Jas had gotten me this interview in the first place. I could do this.

"Listen, as much as I love watching you play for the Warriors, I gotta say, Colorado looks good on you," Chet said. "Just pack your bags, man, and come on down. We got a team here that needs better defense. And we got clear mountain air and a Rocky Mountain high." He gave another thumbs-up and laughed at his own joke. "I know a few guys at the SnowCaps. Want me to get you a phone number?"

I felt myself smile, something I never did in interviews. "Their defense is fine, they just need to deploy it better. And they need a different offensive strategy."

"I'm definitely getting you that phone number, man. This season, they need all the help they can get."

Twenty minutes later, the interview was over. We'd talked about my career, my injuries, even the fact that I was dating my high school sweetheart, which was all over social media. The world had decided that the photo of Jasmine in my lap was now cute instead of offensive. Jasmine said it was now a meme, which I did not understand. She'd tried to explain it to me three times.

I usually hated interviews, but this one felt easy. As I left the studio, nodding to the friendly people thanking me, I wondered why. Was it because of Chet Brett? Was it because it was Denver, so close to my hometown? Was something different about me?

Then, in the lobby, I caught sight of her. Jasmine was waiting for me, her cheeks red from the cold outside, the case for her AirPods in her hand. "It went perfect!" she said, clapping her hands together in excitement when she saw me. "I heard every word! I am so proud of you!"

This, I realized, was why it had been easy.

I didn't say a word to her. Instead, right there in the lobby, I swung her up into my arms, one arm under her shoulders and the other under her knees. Jasmine gave a whoop of surprise, then hooked an arm around my neck.

She waved her free hand at the people who were staring at us as I carried her out the door. "Bye! Have a nice day! Merry Christmas!"

THERE WAS GOING to be a big event at the inn and tree farm on Christmas Eve, two days away. Jasmine was helping to plan it, dealing with caterers and musicians. I'd agreed to a skate on the pond with kids, which only made me slightly nervous. I liked kids, and they liked me, but I was a lot bigger than they were. If one of them collided with me, it would be game over.

I did another interview, this one with a local journalist for a Salt Springs newspaper site. I talked up the Christmas Eve event like Jasmine had told me to, getting the word out that it was happening, it was free, and I would be there. The weather was going to be clear, cold, and perfect. We wanted a crowd.

Jasmine didn't come with me this time—she was too busy. So

when the interview finished, I stopped at a local coffee shop and picked up her favorite drink. Then I went to her apartment, where she was working.

She answered my knock wearing a T-shirt, a pair of women's boxers, and nothing else. Her hair was tied up messily and the distracted look on her face cleared up when she saw me. "You're here! How did the interview go?"

"Fine." I held the cup out to her. "This is for you."

"It is?" She took it and sipped as I came through the door and closed it behind me. "Oh my God, it's a mint mocha."

"Isn't that your favorite?" It had been in high school.

"It's absolutely my favorite." She pulled me down to her and kissed me. She tasted like mint mocha. I kissed her again, deeper this time.

She pulled away after a long moment. "I'm supposed to be working," she said, her voice wavering.

"Don't let me interrupt."

Jas looked unsure, but she took her cup back to the tiny desk where her laptop sat. I pulled up the room's only chair and sat down.

I felt like I took up half the apartment. Jas's bachelor was tiny, with a bed in the corner behind a screen, her table and laptop, a single chair in front of a TV, and a kitchen along the far wall. It was definitely the apartment of a divorced woman who was just getting by. It was cozy, but every time I was in here, I felt like a bull in a china shop about to knock something over.

"Did you see your Instagram?" Jasmine asked. "The pictures from the photo shoot have been a huge hit. The inn is now booked solid through New Year's."

"That's good," I said. I didn't want to talk too much, because she was supposed to be working.

But instead of working, she kept talking. "I've got so much done for the party. I made a signup form for the kids and put it online. That way the parents can sign the waiver ahead of time and we know how many kids to expect. We'll have to limit the number so the ice isn't too crowded."

"Okay," I said.

"Are you going to teach the kids some techniques? Or maybe shoot pucks with them? Gently, of course." She took a sip of her mocha.

"Whatever you want," I replied.

That made her lips curve in a smile. "I like the sound of that."

I narrowed my eyes at her. "I told you, I'm all yours. You're in charge."

Her gaze got a little unfocused and she bit her lip, unaware she was doing it.

"Don't you have work to do?" I prompted her.

"What? Oh, right. Work." She glanced at her laptop. "I'm supposed to be working."

"Maybe you should take a break." I slid my gaze down to her perfect legs, bare in those boxer shorts. Her toes were painted Christmas red. We kept getting distracted by sex, and I couldn't stop it. I didn't want to stop it, because I couldn't get enough of her. How Jasmine managed to be sexy and adorable at the same time, I would never know. Apparently, it was my catnip.

The way she was looking at me said I was her catnip, too. Me, with my giant body, my beard, and my aches and pains everywhere. No woman had looked at me like Jasmine did—not just greedy, but as if she actually liked me. I honestly didn't care what any other woman thought about me, ever again.

"A break?" she asked, her voice a little breathy.

Oh, hell yes. Without another word, I stood and pressed her laptop closed. Then I picked her up—bad back be damned, I loved picking Jasmine up, my arms full of soft, warm woman—and dropped her on the bed.

She squealed, but her look was definitely hazy now, and her

body went limp. I slid my hands up her hips, and in seconds I had pulled off her boxers and panties, leaving her only in a T-shirt.

"I can't," she whispered, her voice husky. She waved a hand vaguely toward her desk. "Work..."

"Ten minutes." I lowered to my knees to the floor, pulling her to the edge of the bed. "Actually, I'm going to torture you. Make it fifteen."

I spread her thighs apart, baring her to me, and her lips parted, her cheeks going red. "Oh, my God," she choked out. "I think I love it when you're bossy."

"Good. We're going out for dinner later. After work." I got into position. "But first, we'll do this."

"Matt!"

I lowered my mouth.

She stopped protesting.

I took twenty minutes. I like to take my time.

TWENTY-TWO

Jasmine

I STARED AT MY PHONE, unable to stop the smile on my face. The photo on Instagram was one of the cutest things I'd ever seen—and it was of Matt and me.

It had. been taken outside an Italian restaurant in downtown Salt Springs. Matt and I had just left after dinner at the restaurant, and we were walking on the sidewalk, which was covered in fresh snow. The shot was from behind, showing Matt in his dark wool coat, his body enormous, and me next to him, wearing my parka and a red wool hat. I remembered that moment—we were heading for his car, and I'd briefly lost my balance in the slippery snow. With his lightning reflexes, Matt had reached out a hand and gripped mine in my red mitten, helping me get my balance. The photo showed the two of us walking on the snowy sidewalk, my hand in his as I laughed. Matt was smiling at me, one of his real smiles that made him unbearably gorgeous.

It had been a perfect moment, and apparently someone who

recognized us had taken a shot of it. The Instagram post was by a user I didn't recognize, and the caption read: *Saw this on the street last night and OMG these two are SO CUTE!! I love them together so much!!* It was followed by a string of emojis.

There were hundreds of comments. I scrolled through them.

They need to get married right noooooowwwww

Ugh why can't that be me? Matt Kringle is the hottest man on the planet

This just melted me!

Who is she? I want to hate her but I can't do it.

HOW is he that hot??? Like how??

Is that the girl who was on his lap? I hope so!

Okay fine, if Matt Kringle has to have a girlfriend, I guess she'll do.

When does he play again? He is the GOAT!

Who is she??

I have never seen him smile like that!

I like her better than Astrid Peachtree. She dumped him. Not cool!

Wait Matt Kringle has a girlfriend? Nooooo

They would make beautiful babies!

The picture had gone viral, getting reposted to other accounts. It had also made it to Twitter, where it was being retweeted everywhere.

Okay, it was a little bit weird, being commented about on the internet. But not all of them were wrong. Matt *was* incredibly hot. And we would make really nice babies.

I felt a flush through my entire body at that thought. What was wrong with me? I had never been baby-crazy before. Was it because I was thirty-four and the biological clock was a real thing? I had always thought it was a made-up cliché.

Or was it the Matt effect? Was his testosterone wafting over me in a powerful cloud, making me think of getting knocked up?

Could men actually do that to you? The thought was terrifying and thrilling at the same time.

"Jasmine?"

I looked up from my phone to see Penelope Gold, one of the CEOs of the Kane Christmas Company, smiling at me. I was standing outside the entrance to the Kringle Inn and Christmas Tree Farm, leaning against my car door. I had just been getting out of my car when I got distracted by social media and forgotten where I was.

Penelope had her curly hair tucked up under a knit cap. She was the kind of woman who looked really pretty in glasses. She was wearing an ankle-length dress under her winter coat.

"We're done with the decorations," she told me. "Just putting up the finishing touches now."

"Great!" I said. We had partnered with Kane Co. to decorate the farm for tonight's party. In exchange for decorating, the ornament company got to advertise for free and put in a booth selling their beautiful, locally made ornaments.

"It should be fun," Penelope said. "Wesley and I will try to come."

Right. Wesley Kane was Kane Co.'s other CEO and Penelope's husband. He looked a lot like Chris Pine. There was just something in the Colorado air that made men gorgeous here. "I hope you make it," I said, and then my gaze dropped to where her winter coat was unzipped. That was when I noticed that Penelope had a round, tidy belly sticking out.

I pressed my lips together. I was not going to comment. What if she had just eaten a pizza? That belly could be pizza, not—

Penelope laughed. "I can see you trying not to ask. Yes, I'm pregnant. I'm five months along."

"Oh!" I said, relieved. "Okay, then! That's great. Congratulations!"

"Thanks." She smiled, and she was so glowingly happy it

made me smile back. Babies. The world was determined to put babies everywhere I looked.

When Penelope was gone, I walked into the tree farm and looked around. Kane Co. had gone all out—everywhere I looked were pine boughs, sprigs of holly, beautiful tinsel garlands, and ornaments. One of the trees from the tree farm had been placed in the middle of the open space and covered with lights and ornaments. More strings of lights were everywhere, and I knew that after dark this place would be magical.

It was perfect, and because of the deal I'd made with Penelope, it hadn't cost anything from our budget. I was *good* at this. Really, really good.

I took a deep breath, taking in the crisp, winter air, and finally felt like I had put it all behind me—the divorce, the string of bad luck in my career. Despite a rocky start, the Kringle job had gone perfectly, and thanks to Matt's mention of me in his statement, I already had two new clients for the New Year, as well as meetings with more potential clients. My January was going to be incredibly busy—and profitable.

I was going to kick ass next year, which was great. Then I thought about Penelope's baby bump again, and wondered how I could work that in for myself, too. What if I decided I wanted more, then went for it?

The sky was the limit. Anything was possible.

Tonight was going to be amazing.

TWENTY-THREE

Matt

CHILDREN. There were so, so many children.

We had ended up with a dozen kids on the list for the skate at the party, which doesn't sound like a lot. But when they were all between five and twelve, and all of them were on skates, going in all directions, it felt like a lot of kids. Like, hundreds.

A little boy was crying, and two of the older kids were about to get into a fistfight. An Asian girl of about eight, who was a better skater than the rest of them, was doing circles on the pond. The parents were standing at the pond's edge, clapping and cheering on their kids, distracting them. And I stood in the middle of the ice, wearing my Warriors jersey with stick in hand, getting completely ignored. I had to get my shit together.

All through the grounds, people were enjoying themselves. I could hear laughter and music. The sun was setting, and the Christmas lights were coming on to illuminate the twilight. It was Christmas Eve. It was magical.

I did not feel magical.

I felt sick to my stomach.

An hour before I got on the ice, I'd gotten a phone call. After months of near radio silence, the call was from the Chicago Warriors. They wanted me back in Chicago for an emergency meeting. Tonight.

They'd wanted me to go to the airport right away, but I'd said no. I couldn't bail on tonight's skate and disappoint not only Jasmine but a bunch of innocent kids. I'd explained that for me to cancel the appearance would be terrible publicity—Matt Kringle, the man who abandons children on Christmas Eve—and they'd relented just enough to book me a flight later in the evening.

The meeting was important enough to happen on Christmas Eve, and the NHL wouldn't be put off. My agent told me I had no choice if I wanted to keep my career. So the end result was that my bags were already packed, I needed to be at the airport in two hours, and Jasmine knew nothing about it.

To say I was not in a jovial mood was an understatement.

"Listen up!" I barked at the kids wreaking chaos around me, my voice carrying over the ice. "Here's how this is gonna go!"

The kids stopped, looking at me with wide eyes.

"You!" I pointed to one kid, then another. "You, you, you! All of you there! You're Team One. Line up to the left. The rest of you are Team Two. Line up to the right. Over there. Now, got it?"

It worked. The kids, even the crying one and the lightning-fast eight-year-old, skated into the lines I'd directed.

"Okay. Stick handling!" I shouted. I held up my own stick, demonstrating the grip. "Right hand here. Left hand here. Lefties, you can reverse it. Shoulders back—no hunching. Chin up. Knees bent slightly. Stick to the ice. Go!"

The kids all took position, like a tiny army.

I grabbed one of the pucks I'd brought and held it up. "Puck handling! We're gonna practice. You can't learn to handle the puck when you're in motion if you don't know how to do it standing still. I'm gonna start with this kid here." I pointed to a kid at the end of his row, who was about ten and looked vaguely terrified. "You," I said to him. "I'm gonna drop the puck in front of you, and you shoot it to the kid across from you." I pointed to the Asian girl, who was positioned across from the first boy. "You shoot to the next kid. Back and forth. Everyone still, no skating. Got it?"

"I can skate and shoot," the girl argued back at me.

I pointed at her. "No skating. You skate, it's a foul and you sit in the penalty box until I say you can leave. Got it?"

She stuck her tongue out, but she obeyed.

I dropped the puck in front of the first kid, and he passed to the girl. She passed to the next kid. Back and forth, the puck moved across the ice like a braid.

"Too slow!" I shouted when the puck had come to every kid. "Go back the other way. Faster!"

They did it faster, and then I had them take turns shooting while skating at the net I'd set up. I kept it simple—I didn't make them do any of the speed or agility drills I had to do regularly in practice. They were here to have some fun, not puke with exhaustion like I'd done more times than I could count.

When each of them had shot at the net, I started the final play of the game. The kids were all rapt now, their attention on me. Even the parents were quiet, and no one was distracted.

I pulled a goalie helmet out of my duffel bag and put it under my arm, then skated in front of the net. "Now," I told them, "you take turns trying to get the puck past me. You see how big I am?" I jerked a thumb at the net. "You see how small this is? You got your work cut out for you. Let's see who's got what it takes." I put the helmet on, lowered the face guard, and assumed a goalie crouch. "Let's fucking go."

And they did. Laughing, challenging each other, high-fiving

each other, cheering each other on, each kid took a turn shooting the puck at me. If any of the parents objected to my language, none of them had the balls to call me on it. I wouldn't have listened anyway.

The kids were having so much fun that we did a second round of taking shots on goal. Then I signed autographs and took a few pictures.

I was almost late for my flight. I unlaced my skates in record time, dumping my gear into my duffel bag. I looked around but didn't see Jasmine anywhere. She must be crazy busy, helping to run the party.

I'd just have to text her goodbye. There was no time.

I had to meet with the NHL, and I had to do it tonight. Maybe they had something important to say to me. But more importantly, I had something to say to them. There was no point putting it off. I'd say what I had to say to them as soon as I got off the plane.

I put on my boots and my coat, hefted my bag, and left from the back of the lot, headed for my rental car and Chicago.

TWENTY-FOUR

Jasmine

CHRISTMAS DAY WAS BEAUTIFUL. The sky was blue, the air was clear, and there was pristine, white snow on the ground. The mountains in the distance only added to the wonder of it. All of Salt Springs was festive.

At least, I assumed it was. From my spot in bed, under my covers, I couldn't see.

I lay in the dark, my knees curled up, my hair a mess. I'd watched a nonstop *Parks and Rec* marathon until three o'clock in the morning, and I'd barely gotten any sleep. Now I was tired, sad, and my girl-crush on Amy Poehler was worse than ever.

Last night's party had been a huge success. The entire Kringle campaign had been a huge success. Judging by my inbox, my business was about to be a huge success. And all I wanted to do was lie here, under my covers, and never come out again.

I'd seen Matt start his skate with the kids last night, and then I'd been distracted, dealing with party details. When I'd gone back an hour later, the rink was empty. The kids were gone. Matt was gone.

As I'd stood there, cold and confused, my phone had pinged with a text. It was Matt. *NHL called. I have to go to Chicago tonight. I'll call you with news as soon as I have it.*

Just like that. *NHL called.* And Matt was gone out of my life, back to his life as a hockey player.

I'd had a taste, in that moment, of what it had felt like for Matt when I broke up with him so suddenly in high school. I remembered the look on his face, and I'd wondered if I had the same look on mine. It was horrible, that feeling. I was sorry I'd ever made him feel it. I was sorry that I had to feel it now. I was just sorry, period.

Things had been going so good. How had I let myself slip? I knew that Matt wasn't in Salt Springs forever. I knew that anything we started would be short-term. I'd tried to resist. But then I'd fallen into his lap, and then he'd kissed me, and somehow I'd ended up stripping naked? The details were fuzzy, because my mind was hazy with lust. Okay—maybe not just lust. Maybe I was completely crazy about him, too.

But somehow, in this tangle of love and lust, I'd had incredible sex for the first time in my life, not just once but over and over again. I'd felt beautiful and valued and sexy and truly cared for, instead of like I was playing a role, as I had when I was married. I'd thought about babies. I'd followed my heart. I'd stopped thinking about Matt leaving, until I was standing by the edge of the pond after it had already happened.

I groaned. "This is stupid!" I said aloud into my bubble under the blankets. "He's just a man. I don't need a man."

I didn't. Leslie Knope would agree. The problem was, I liked this particular man. A man was nice to have when he came in the form of Matt Kringle.

I was thinking about turning on *Parks and Rec* again when

my phone rang, lighting up the darkness. The call display said it was my brother, Brad. I punched the button to answer on speaker so I wouldn't have to lift my hand to my ear.

"Hello?" I croaked.

"What's up, J-Town?" Brad said. "Yo, it's Christmas. We're due to see the 'rents in an hour."

This was my brother, the former Salt Springs High football player. He was pushing forty, if you could believe it, and he still said things like "yo" and called our parents "the 'rents."

"Stop calling me J-Town," I said.

"Why? It's your name."

"It's a nickname you gave me when we were teenagers, and it's never made any sense."

"Whoa, J-Town, you're in a bad mood. What up? It's Christmas. Is it your time of the month or something?"

I closed my eyes, wishing for patience. My brother was an insurance broker who had a girlfriend with two kids, but his maturity level hadn't progressed much past age sixteen. "I'm just having a bad day, that's all."

"Well, come to Mom and Dad's, then. Mom's cooking up her big turkey dinner and Dad's planning to watch *It's a Wonderful Life*. It'll be sick."

"Brad, you're too old to call things sick. It's a law or something."

"No way. Age is just a number. What's got you so down, anyway?"

I had no reason to tell my stupid brother anything, but I'd been alone for too long. "It's my love life," I said. "Do you remember Matt Kringle?"

"Do I remember him? Of course, man! He's a legend. I hear he's in town this week. You should try and call him up or something, since you two used to date. Maybe we could go for a beer. That would be amazing. I love that guy."

"You love him? You barely talked to him in high school! You called him a moron!"

"That's because he played hockey," Brad said, completely unapologetic. "We football guys had to kick the hockey players' asses. But man, did Kringle ever turn out to be a killer hockey player. Just amazing. What does he have to do with your bad mood?"

"I'm in a bad mood because I was in love with him when I was seventeen." The words came out in an avalanche, and I couldn't stop them. "I broke up with him because I was afraid he'd break my heart. And then he came back because I asked him to, even though he had good reason to hate me. And even though he jerseyed his brother in the airport, it was amazing to be with him again. He got a giant candy cane and I fell in his lap, and we had to fake date, except it was real. We were really dating. And he skated in the cold so I could take pictures and put them on his Instagram, and I fell in love with him all over again. Like really in love. And now the NHL called him back and he's gone. And my heart got broken anyway, so there was no point in breaking up with him in the first place."

There was a long pause. The only reason I knew that Brad was still on the line was because my phone's display said he was.

"Brad?" I said.

"Um, okay," Brad said slowly. "I didn't understand the parts about jerseys or candy canes, but it sounds like you got back together with Kringle while he was in town and now he's gone back to the Warriors."

That was pretty concise, especially for Brad. "Something like that, yes."

"Let me ask you this. Did he dump you?"

I blinked my tired eyes, which felt like they were made of sandpaper. "He texted me that he had to go back to Chicago, and he'd call me later."

"Okay, so he didn't dump you. You know, like tell you to get lost, it's over."

"No," I admitted.

Brad sighed. "Look J-Town, I know you know nothing about sports, so let me fill you in. Him getting a call from the NHL is a big deal. Like, they're paying Kringle millions of dollars, and at this point they're paying him not to play. If they call him and tell him to go back to Chicago, it's serious. He has to go. Even if he doesn't want to."

"I know," I said. "I know he has to go. But Brad, this isn't going to work. They're calling him back to put him on the ice again."

"Good, because the Warriors need better defense. They need to clinch that Playoff spot."

"You don't get it. Matt is going to go back to his amazing NHL life, and he's never coming back to Salt Springs again. You think a guy like that wants to live in this town, with a nobody like me? He's going to forget about me in ten minutes. It's never going to work."

"You sell yourself short, sis," Brad said. "You're a smokeshow. All my friends in high school always said so."

"Oh, gross." Brad's friends were all football players, and for most of them the elevator didn't go all the way to the top floor of the building, if you know what I mean. Plus, they were Brad's friends. Just no.

"Well, I wasn't gonna let them date you. Come on. But you're pretty and you're hot and you're smart and everyone likes you. Kringle is lucky if he locks that down, and I'm not just saying that because I'm your brother."

"But you always liked Gareth," I said.

"Sure, Green was boss in high school, but he turned out to be a dipshit. He's not cool anymore. Now, Matt Kringle? He's fuckin' cool. He's almost good enough for you. Almost."

I sighed. "Brad, that's the nicest thing you've ever said to me."

"Sure. You know that lots of NHL players are married, right? They make it work. It happens all the time."

Married? It was a little too soon to be thinking about that. Matt needed to call me back first. Then we needed to talk about babies, because apparently I was obsessed. Then, maybe, we'd talk about marriage.

I'd had enough of weddings to last me a long time.

"Okay," I said to my brother. "You've made me feel better. A little."

"Good."

"Thank you."

"No problem, J-Town," Brad said. "It'll all work out. It's Christmas. Turkey fixes everything. Get dressed."

TWENTY-FIVE

Jasmine

BRAD, for once in his life, was right. Turkey did make my mood better. So did a day with my family, even though they drove me crazy and my mom lamented how single I was and we ended up playing Monopoly because Dad wanted to. Dad always wanted to play Monopoly, because Dad always won. He was ruthless.

Matt didn't call.

At ten that night I made my way home, moving slowly because of all the food I'd eaten—I'd worn stretchy pants and a sweatshirt to my parents' because I wasn't born yesterday. In my apartment, I toed my shoes off and lay back on my bed, wondering if I would be able to eat again anytime before next Thanksgiving.

I was lying there, drifting into turkey-induced dreamland, when my phone rang. I picked it up. It was Matt.

My heart jumped in my chest, and I answered. "Hello?"

"I didn't call," Matt said, his voice rough. "I'm sorry."

"Oh," I said, some of my worry disappearing at the sound of his voice. "Okay."

"I didn't say goodbye when I left, either. There was no time. I'm sorry about that, too."

I blinked. "Well, it would have been nice, but I understand."

"I had to catch a plane. And if I said goodbye to you, I'd never go. Because I didn't want to leave."

Now my heart, which was already pounding, did a sweet little lurch. "I didn't want you to leave, either," I admitted. "I wouldn't have let you go."

"You see? I had to do it quick. Like a Band-Aid. But I'm still sorry."

He didn't sound relaxed and full, like I was. He hadn't spent the day with his family. He'd left his family on Christmas Eve to be a thousand miles away, all alone.

"What did the NHL want with you?" I asked him.

"Meetings," Matt said. "Meetings and then phone calls. Lots of phone calls."

"Even on Christmas Day?"

"The NHL doesn't take a break at this time of year."

Of course not. This was Matt the Mountain possibly coming back to play—there would be phone calls about that, no matter what day it was. And there weren't any games played on Christmas Day, but in two days there were ten games being played across the league, a fact I knew because I couldn't help googling it in my parents' kitchen after I cleared the dinner dishes. The Warriors were scheduled to play in Vancouver. If Matt was going to be in the game, he'd be getting on a plane soon.

"So I guess you should pack," I said.

"For what?"

"Vancouver."

There was a brief pause. "I'm not going to play in Vancouver."

"Oh, right, of course." I sat up. "One of the articles I read said that you'd have to be assessed by the team doctors before you're cleared to play. And if you're cleared, the team might give you a week to train. So you'll be playing by New Year's, which means either the home game on New Year's Eve, or the Winter Classic, which is back in Buffalo this year."

"Jasmine," Matt said. "The fact that you're talking hockey right now is very, very sexy."

"It is?" This surprised me. I wasn't trying to be sexy. In fact, sitting here in my stretchy clothes, full of turkey, I was the opposite. "I might have looked up a few things."

"A few things?"

"I couldn't help it. Monopoly is boring. I spend a lot of time in jail. Another article said that the reason you're such a great player is that you combine size and speed like no other player. It said that when you're on the ice, it seems impossible that a man so big could be both so fast and so agile. It also said that you're able to come up with strategies on the fly, as you're skating, and your opponents never know what you're going to do next. I thought that was fascinating."

"Holy shit." Matt's voice sounded strained. "I think I've just found the most heavenly dirty talk I've ever heard."

I was smiling, and I couldn't stop. "The article said that you have extraordinary strength, flexibility, and reflexes. In my expert opinion, I agree."

"Jasmine."

"Are you naked?"

"One minute." There was a shuffling sound. "Now I am."

Now I was picturing it, and it wasn't a fantasy this time. I was recalling it from memory. It was *amazing*. "This is really turning you on?" I asked.

"Fuck, yes. Keep going."

"Offside," I said. "Blue line. Penalty box." I wasn't entirely sure what any of those meant, but I was going to learn. If my boyfriend, the one I was in love with, was a hockey player, then I'd be a hockey expert, stat. "Power play."

"Oh, baby." Then we were both laughing, unable to help ourselves. And oh, gosh. Matt didn't laugh often, and I loved the sound so much. I loved *him* so much.

"Get your mind out of the gutter for just a minute, Jasmine," Matt said. "We have to talk business. I need to explain some things."

"You really don't," I said. "I get it. I was hurt at first, but you're an NHL player. You're amazing at what you do, and you love it. If I have to be a hockey girlfriend, then I can be a hockey girlfriend. At least, I'm willing to try."

There was a brief pause. "You're trying to kill me," he said, his voice choked. "I don't deserve you. Not even for a fucking second."

"You do, though," I said. Tears burned my eyes, but I wouldn't let them fall. "You deserve someone who loves you and has your back, not someone who's the same height as you. That's me. And I deserve someone like that, too. I really, really do. And I think that person is you."

"It is me," Matt said. "I love you, Jas. Part of me has been in love with you since the day you told me to ask you out in English class."

"Why do you think I sat next to you?" I asked, sniffing. The tears were falling despite my best efforts. "I thought you were awesome. And I was right."

"You don't have to be a hockey girlfriend. Not like you think."

I wiped the tears from my cheeks. "Why? Because I won't get a boob job? I draw the line at that. It would make me look stupid."

"What?" Matt sounded confused. "No one is asking you to get a boob job. I mean you don't have to be a hockey girlfriend because I'm not playing hockey anymore."

I froze, my hand still on my cheek. "What?"

"It's why I came back for these meetings," he said. "The team wanted to talk about when I can play again, but I wanted to talk about the other job offer I got."

"What job offer?"

"On the coaching staff for the Colorado SnowCaps," Matt said. "They're based in Denver. Which means I can move to Salt Springs and make it my home. With you."

The breath had left my chest, and for a second I was so surprised I could barely speak. "But Matt—don't you want to play? Isn't that what you've always loved?"

"Why do people always ask me that?" he grumbled. "Yes, I love to play hockey. Of course I do. But it's a fucking game. I did it for a long time, and it was great. But my body is telling me to slow down. The message is loud and clear, and if I don't listen, I'm going to get an injury that shuts me down for good." I shuddered, thinking about the scare with his neck. "So I'll coach. It's my turn to stand at the edge of the ice and yell at guys instead of getting yelled at. Besides, hockey isn't a person to come home to at the end of the day. You are. So I'll coach hockey in Denver, and at the end of the day I'll come home. To you."

I was crying and swooning at the same time. I couldn't believe this was real. "I want kids," I blurted.

Matt didn't miss a beat. "You do? You're sure?"

"I'm sure." I so was. "I want them soon."

"Jas, that's fine with me. If I wasn't in Chicago, I'd knock you up right now."

"Not right now," I said. "I have to digest this turkey dinner first."

"Then I'll do it as soon as I fucking can."

"Okay." I sniffed. "I'll hold you to that."

"Jasmine." Matt's voice was quiet, serious. "Before I do all of this, tell me straight, because I have to know. Are you in?"

I knew what he was asking. Was I in for all of it? The great things, the terrible things, the scary things? Kids and careers and the messy parts of life? It was going to be wonderful, I knew that. But it wasn't going to be easy. I knew that, too.

"I'm in," I said, my voice shaking. "I love you, Matt. I'm in."

He sighed, and it was a great sound. The sound of him trusting me.

"Okay," he said. "Wait for me, Jasmine. I'll be home as soon as I can."

EPILOGUE

Jasmine

New Year's Eve

It was a cold, clear night, and the snow crunched under my boots when I got out of the car. The stars were icy pinpoints in the sky, and the light coming from the windows of the Kringle family home were warm and bright. I inhaled a deep breath of crisp, perfect air.

Matt got out of the passenger's side and came around the car to stand next to me. He loomed huge in the near-dark. "Ready?" he asked in his deep rumble.

I felt the vibrations of that voice in my whole body. I'd picked him up at the airport two hours ago. We'd fought traffic all the way to Salt Springs, where he dropped his suitcase in my tiny apartment. Then we'd had a hot, energetic reunion on my bed, this time without any Chicago Warriors condoms. Pure bliss.

We'd stayed in bed until the last possible minute, when we were almost late. Then we'd gotten dressed again and come to his family house.

"My family is a bit much," Matt warned me, his hands in the pockets of his wool coat.

"I like them," I said.

"And yet you're still standing here and not going in."

I bit my lip. I really liked all of Matt's family, but this was kind of a big deal. The two of us as a couple, doing a family gathering thing. Oh, and there was a possibility I was pregnant as of an hour ago. No pressure or anything!

Matt took a hand from his pocket and put it gently on the back of my neck, his touch warm. I practically purred. "You'll do fine," he said softly. "Everyone loves you." He paused. "*I love you.*"

I felt my throat close up. Matt had taken a beating in the sports media for the supposed betrayal of his team when he took the coaching job. It made me angry, but Matt said the articles were just for clicks. *The team is fine with it,* he said. *I already talked to all of them. It's what I've spent the past week doing.*

That was the Matt I knew—the guy who would talk to his team about leaving, the guy who took a coaching job to be near me and start a family. The guy who told me he loved me. He might be rough, but everyone was so, so wrong about him.

"I love you, too," I said, taking his hand from the back of my neck and kissing his palm. "You're going to be a great dad."

"Let's not get ahead of ourselves," he grunted. "I'm planning on a few months of trying. That part is fun."

I agreed. I smiled and tugged his hand. "It's cold out here. Let's go in."

Before we could, the front door flew open. "What are you doing out here, little brother?" Ethan said. "Get in here. You're late."

He was wearing jeans and a navy blue sweater that fit him perfectly. His hair was mussed in the most awesome way and his blue eyes twinkled as he gave us a grin.

"We're coming," Matt said, climbing the step. He squinted at his brother. "Are those jeans new? Like brand new? They still have fold marks."

"They are. Do you like this outfit?" Ethan smoothed a hand over the sweater. "Lexie bought it for me."

On cue, Lexie's head popped up over Ethan's shoulder. Her blond hair was tied in a messy knot on top of her head and her dangly earrings sparkled. From inside the house, her dog, Baby Girl, started barking. "Jas!" she said to me.

"Lexie!" I ran up the steps, past Ethan, toward her. We hugged like long-lost sisters, even though I had just seen her yesterday when we went shopping together.

Lexie was staying in Salt Springs, and we were going to be besties. We already were.

"Do you like these?" she asked when our hug was done, shaking her head so her crystal earrings moved. "They're from a show I did five years ago. We all had to wear them, and the lights were designed to make them sparkle all the way to the back row. I thought they were appropriate for New Year's."

"They're awesome," I said as I slid off my coat.

"I hope you're hungry." This was Kristen, coming down the hall toward us. She was wearing pants of soft, drapey cloth and a cropped sweater. Her dark hair was down, brushed softly over her shoulders, and she was smiling. "Paul and I have been cooking all day."

"I don't recall you cooking," Paul's voice shouted from the kitchen. "I do recall you eating, though."

"I put the salad together!" Kristen called back. "I definitely chopped an onion! And I was awesome at it." She turned back to me and hugged me. Then she stepped up to Matt and kissed him on the cheek.

Matt's eyes went wide. "What's happened to you?" he asked. "I don't think you've kissed me since third grade. And that time was because you lost a bet with Ethan."

"It was her or me," Ethan agreed. "I'm glad I won."

"I'm nice now," Kristen said, giving both of her brothers a glare. "I mean it. I'm really nice. Get used to it."

"Yes, ma'am," Ethan said.

"Absolutely," Matt agreed.

"Let's get a drink," Lexie said.

We moved to the kitchen. Paul was taking something from the oven that looked a lot like—"Is that lasagna?" I asked.

"Yes, it is." He smiled at me, his teeth white behind his beard. He wore an apron that said *Kiss the cook*, and underneath it he wore jeans and a flannel shirt, as if he had just come from the tree farm. The oven mitts on his hands had reindeer faces on them.

"*Homemade* lasagna?" This was amazing. Who made lasagna from scratch instead of buying it? Apparently Paul did.

"I put together the salad," Kristen said again, and Paul put an arm around her waist, kissing her.

Sitting in a chair in the corner of the kitchen was Chris Kringle, his crutches next to him and his broken leg stretched out. His white hair was brushed neatly back and he was wearing a button-down shirt, probably the only one he owned. "I tasted the sauce when he made it," he said. "I tasted the desserts, too. Everything is really good."

Everything *was* good. We ate and talked, because there was so much to talk about. Kristen and Lexie were taking over running the inn so that Chris could retire. Chris's cast was coming off in a week. Ethan was going to run for mayor. Paul was still running the tree farm, and he was going to start offering some horticulture classes. Lexie was living at Ethan's, and Kristen and

Paul were living in their cabin, which they were finishing and decorating.

And Matt and me? We were going house-hunting, starting tomorrow. We were going to get our own place here in Salt Springs. Things were going to be busy for a few months as Matt flew back and forth from Chicago, wrapping up his life there and starting his life here with me. It was going to be crazy. It was also going to be a lot of fun.

I was lining up new clients for my PR business, and I would work for the Kringle Inn and Christmas Tree Farm when they needed me—like for the Valentine's Day party Lexie was throwing at the inn and for the haunted house she was already planning for Halloween.

When the food was gone and the dishes had been cleared, I slipped out the back door for a breath of fresh air. Alone in the quiet, the snow under my feet, I looked up at the stars.

Matt came out after me. Without a word, he put his big arms around me from behind, pulling me into his warm chest. Holding me. Keeping me warm.

Inside, everyone started to count down. *Ten, nine, eight...*

When they hit *one*, Matt lowered his head and kissed the side of my neck, his beard brushing my skin. "Happy New Year, Jasmine," he said softly.

"I love you," I said, leaning back into him. "It's going to be amazing."

And it was.